Sprinkle SUNDAYS

ICE CREAM
SANDWICHED

Coco Simon

Simon Spotlight

New York   London   Toronto   Sydney   New Delhi

SIMON SPOTLIGHT
An imprint of Simon & Schuster Children's Publishing Division
1230 Avenue of the Americas, New York, New York 10020
This Simon Spotlight edition October 2018
Copyright © 2018 by Simon & Schuster, Inc.
All rights reserved, including the right of reproduction in whole or in part in any form.
SIMON SPOTLIGHT and colophon are registered trademarks of Simon & Schuster, Inc.
For information about special discounts for bulk purchases, please contact Simon & Schuster Special Sales at 1-866-506-1949 or business@simonandschuster.com.
Text by Tracey West
Series designed by Hannah Frece
Cover designed by Alisa Coburn and Hannah Frece
Cover illustrations by Alisa Coburn
The text of this book was set in Bembo Std.
Manufactured in the United States of America 0918 OFF
10 9 8 7 6 5 4 3 2 1
ISBN 978-1-5344-2449-4 (hc)
ISBN 978-1-5344-2448-7 (pbk)
ISBN 978-1-5344-2450-0 (eBook)
Library of Congress Catalog Card Number 2018948332

CHAPTER ONE
A REALLY BIG DEAL

I put the finishing touches on my book review as the school bus pulled into Vista Green School.

"Perfect Pairing," I typed into my tablet. "Eat a scoop of banana ice cream sprinkled with toasted coconut to taste the flavors of Barbados. Although, I'm pretty sure that the Puritans did not approve of ice cream!"

Puritans, ice cream, and Barbados. Okay, that sounded a little weird. But I'd selected *The Witch of Blackbird Pond* as my first book to review for the school newspaper, the *Green Gazette*. I'd chosen it because I'd thought it would be good to start with a classic, and this book had won an award (a Newbery Medal, which was a big deal for books). *The Witch of*

Blackbird Pond was about a girl from Barbados who, in the 1600s, moved to New England and had to adapt to a Puritan lifestyle. I'd checked to make sure the school library had a copy of it, in case my review inspired anyone to read it.

My new friend Colin was the paper's assistant editor, and it had been his idea for me to add an ice cream pairing to each review. I knew that book reviews didn't usually include food pairings, let alone ice cream suggestions, but my mom just happened to run the newest ice cream parlor in Bayville. Colin knew that I liked to suggest ice cream flavors to customers by asking them about what books they liked. So he'd thought it would be fun to do that as a newspaper column.

I hadn't waited until the last minute on the bus to write the review; I'd tweaked the piece at least seven times already, wanting to make sure it would be perfect before I submitted it to Colin. But today was my deadline, which meant now or never, so I took a deep breath and uploaded it to the shared drive just as the bus came to a stop.

I was still fairly new to Vista Green, and I didn't have any real bus friends yet except for Amanda.

Amanda, her mom, and her sister lived in the same apartment building as my dad. But I got to sit on the bus with her only when I was staying with my dad, and today I was coming from my mom's house.

If that all sounded confusing, that's because it was! My parents had gotten divorced right before I'd started seventh grade, and even though they were being very cool about it all and didn't scream at each other or anything like that, I still hadn't quite adjusted. They had sold our old house in the town we used to live in, and so most days I lived with Mom in a beach bungalow near the ice cream shop, while the other days I lived with Dad in a high-rise apartment with a pool on the roof. It might sound cool to have two houses and two rooms, but I didn't quite feel at home in either place yet.

My new address at the beach house in Bayville also meant that I was going to a different school from my friends, who all went to Martin Luther King Middle School, which was one town away. In my heart, I still felt like I was a student at MLK.

Luckily, I'd managed to make a few friends at Vista Green: Colin, Amanda, and Eloise, who sort of came as a package, I guess. I wouldn't exactly call them nerdy or geeky, but they were definitely not part of the cool club at Vista Green. And by that, I mean that they didn't dress the same and have the same opinions as everyone else, something I'd seen a lot of at my new school.

At least, that was what I'd thought. But that morning, I would learn that the Vista Green Fall Frolic was one event that had just about everybody at the school falling in line.

After I got off the bus, I headed to my locker. For the first time I noticed the Fall Frolic posters plastered on every sage-colored wall I walked past. And everyone was talking about the dance too.

"I have been waiting for this since last year!"

"Did you get your dress yet?"

"I still haven't found the right shoes!"

A few feet away from my locker, I saw Amanda getting her books out of hers.

"Hey, Amanda," I greeted her.

She looked up and smiled, her brown eyes friendly through her black-framed eyeglasses.

"Oh, hey, Allie," she said. "What's up?"

"It seems like everybody is talking about the dance," I said. "Is it a really big deal here?"

I had the bad luck of asking the question just as two girls were passing by: Blair and Palmer. Colin liked to call them the "Witches," but I was starting to think that doing that was insulting to female practitioners of the magical arts. Because there was nothing magical about Blair and Palmer and their other friend, Maria. They were usually just mean—although Blair was by far the worst offender. That was why I had nicknamed the group the "Mean Team."

The girls both stopped in their tracks.

"Is it a big deal?" Palmer repeated, with a flip of her long, straight, brown hair. "It's only the biggest event of the year!" She turned to Blair and asked, "How could she not know that?"

Blair responded with a flip of her own long, straight, sandy-brown hair. "Maybe she's too busy dishing out ice cream at Mommy's store," she said, and then she and Palmer walked away laughing. It actually did kind of sound like cackling, so maybe Colin's assessment was correct.

I was steaming. MLK wasn't perfect, but there I'd had the safe little bubble of friendship with my best friends, Tamiko and Sierra. MLK had a lot of different groups of kids and not one big Cool Club. You

5

could kind of do your own thing, and I'd never had to worry about being a mean-girl victim.

"Well, that was lovely," Amanda said dryly, and then the bell rang.

I headed off to my first class, science with Ms. Conyers. She wasn't my favorite teacher at Vista Green—that would be Ms. Healy, my English teacher. Ms. Conyers was supersmart and kind of reminded me of Ruth Bader Ginsburg, the Supreme Court justice, with her small frame, pulled-back hair, and big eyeglasses. But Ms. Conyers could be a little boring sometimes, even though we were studying Earth's geological history, which should have been really interesting.

It turns out, though, even Ms. Conyers was excited about the Fall Frolic.

"Is anyone in this class on the music committee of the dance?" she asked, and a boy named Logan raised his hand. "Please make sure there aren't too many slow songs this year. I could not get my groove on last fall."

She mimicked a funky dance move, and everyone laughed. Maybe she wasn't as boring as she seemed. As the morning went on, I realized that the Mean Team was right—the dance *was* a big deal. In my next class, Italian with Signore Bianchi, we all learned how to say, "Are you going to the dance?" (*Stai andando al ballo?*) And in art class a small group of kids from the dance committee worked on decorations while the rest of us had our regular lesson.

When it came time for lunch in the cafeteria, I was anxious to get the scoop from my Vista Green friends. Amanda, Colin, Eloise, and I sat at a table with Preston and Haruo, two boys Colin had been friends with since kindergarten. The three of them were, like, best friends, so they usually spent the whole lunch period talking with one another and ignoring us.

"So, the Mean Team set me straight this morning," I began as I unpacked my lunch. Then I filled Colin and Eloise in on what had happened. "I guess this dance really is a big deal."

"Well, first of all, ignore Blair and Palmer, as always," Colin said. "But yeah, I guess it is kind of a big deal here."

Eloise nodded in agreement, her blond curly hair bouncing on her shoulders. "It's a *really* big deal," she said. "Everyone dresses up, and they hire a professional photographer and DJ. It's pretty cool."

Amanda rolled her eyes. "I guess. If you like that kind of thing."

Eloise nudged her. "Oh, come on, Amanda. You like it just as much as everybody else."

Amanda frowned and ate a bite of her sandwich.

"You said everyone dresses up," I said. "Just exactly how dressed up do you mean?"

I was thinking of the sixth-grade dance at MLK, which was pretty casual. A lot of kids just wore jeans and nice shirts. I'd worn a dress and regular flats, but not a fancy dress.

"Well, all the girls shop at that boutique in Upper Springfield," Eloise said, and Amanda rolled her eyes again.

"What boutique?" I asked.

Eloise started tapping on her phone. "It's called Glimmer," she said. "Everyone gets a short dress, not a long one. And everyone gets thin straps."

She showed me a photo on her phone of a model wearing a slinky silver above-the-knee dress with very thin straps. It didn't look like a dress I would ever wear—unless I was going to be walking the Hollywood red carpet. And it definitely didn't look like a dress Mom and Dad were going to let me wear.

"Does *everyone* dress like that?" I asked.

Eloise shrugged. "Most girls. You look out of place if you don't."

"Even you guys?" I asked.

Eloise nodded, and Amanda bit her lower lip.

"It's just . . . I like dancing," Amanda replied. "And this way I don't have to stress about what to wear. I just go to Glimmer and pick something out. It's easy."

"And then we fit in," Eloise added. "Which is not a bad thing, because we don't normally fit in around here."

"I don't know," I said. "That kind of dress is just not . . . my style."

I looked over at Colin, to see if he had an opinion, but he had inserted himself into the conversation between Preston and Haruo. I guessed that the topic of girls' fashion wasn't his favorite.

"You should get over to Glimmer soon," Eloise suggested. "All of the good dresses go early."

"Thanks," I said, and I thoughtfully dug into my salad. Once again I wondered what my life would have been like if my parents hadn't divorced and I were still going to MLK. I knew that the MLK seventh graders got more dressed up for dances than the sixth graders, but I was pretty sure that short, grown-up dresses weren't mandatory.

I sighed. Even if the dresses hadn't been an issue, I knew I was going to miss being at the dance with Sierra and Tamiko. I was glad that I'd met Colin, Amanda, and Eloise. But Amanda and Eloise were best friends already, so I usually felt like a third wheel when just the three of us were together. And Colin was great, but he was a guy—and hanging with Colin was not the same as hanging with my two best girlfriends, whom I could share anything with.

I was so happy that Sierra and Tamiko had agreed to work at my mom's ice cream shop every Sunday. I was guaranteed to spend time with them at least one day a week. But one day a week still didn't feel like enough.

I missed having my Sprinkle Squad around me every day!

CHAPTER TWO
MY DRESS DILEMMA

After school I took the bus back to Mom's house, but I didn't go inside. Instead I made the short walk to Molly's Ice Cream shop, which was pretty much around the corner.

An ocean breeze gave me a slight chill, and I buttoned up my blue cardigan sweater. People had warned me Bayville could get pretty hot in the spring and summer, but fall could get brisk. We'd even had a few days of snow.

Winter still seemed far away on this sunny fall afternoon, and as I walked, I saw some people coming toward me carrying ice cream cones. I smiled, knowing that they had come from my mom's shop. Business could sometimes be slow early in the week, so the cones were a good sign. The business was still new, and I knew Mom was worried about getting things off the ground. It was like the divorce had been only a blip on her radar, and all her energy had been going into Molly's for the past few months.

The reason I was heading to the shop was because we were still figuring out the whole divorced-family thing. Before she'd opened the shop, Mom had been chief financial officer of my dad's company. One of the perks of her working with my dad had been the flexible hours, so she had worked at home in the afternoons and had been there for me and my eight-year-old brother, Tanner, when we'd gotten out of school. Since Dad owned his company, he had to be there for a full day.

Now that Mom ran a business, any hours that she spent away from the shop cost her money, so she had to be at work for a full day too. So for now, the bus dropped Tanner off at the shop after school, and I walked there from my bus stop. Mom said that I was old enough to stay home by myself if I wanted to, but I didn't mind going to the shop when I didn't have any after-school activities. The house was kind of quiet and lonely when I was there by myself. Instead Tanner and I sat at a table in the corner of the shop, and I help him with his homework, and then I worked on mine. I mean, it sounds pretty cool to be able to hang out in an ice cream store every day, but really it was just like being at home, and Mom was unfortunately pretty strict about how much ice cream we could have on a daily basis. Besides, we'd just be eating all her profits.

Some days we stayed at the shop with Mom until she closed, and we just got falafel from Harry's or ordered pizza from Pino's. Other days, Mom left the shop at six and let two college students, Rashid and Daphne, close the shop for her, and she made us dinner. And sometimes, when he could get out early, Dad showed up, took me and Tanner to dinner, and then dropped us off at Mom's house. On the weekends, we stayed at Dad's house, but during the week we usually slept at Mom's. Tanner and I pretty much never knew which kind of day it was going to be until we got to the shop.

"It's a Raphne day," Mom announced when I walked through the door. That meant Rashid and Daphne were closing up the shop. She liked to combine the names "Rashid" and "Daphne" the way some people combined the names of celebrity couples. I didn't think Rashid and Daphne were dating, but it was possible. Sierra had said that there were clearly sparks flying between them, but Sierra loved romantic comedies and tended to see romance when there wasn't any.

"I put a stew in the Crock-Pot this morning," Mom went on.

"Great!" I said, and I walked behind the counter so that she could give me an after-school kiss.

"How was your day?" she asked.

I thought about telling her about the Fall Frolic, but at that moment a gaggle of high school girls came through the door. So I just shrugged and went to my usual corner table. As soon as I sat down, my phone jingled with the sound of an incoming video chat.

I took out my phone to see Sierra and Tamiko pop up on the screen. Sierra had her curly brown hair pulled back into a messy bun, and Tamiko had a pink headband in her sleek black hair. It looked like they were in Tamiko's bedroom.

"Ali Bali!" Tamiko yelled, because she hardly ever called anyone by their real name.

"What's up?" I asked.

"We were just chilling and missing our bestie," Tamiko replied.

"Yeah, MLK stinks without you!" Sierra said.

I sighed. "Sometimes I wish I still went to MLK," I said in a half whisper, so that Mom wouldn't hear me. "Everyone at Vista Green is making a big deal out of the fall dance, and I just don't get it."

"Speaking of dances, we have some news for you," Sierra said. "We asked the teachers in charge of the MLK dance, and they said you could come with us, even if you aren't a student there."

"Seriously?" I replied. "This afternoon I was wishing I could go. You guys know me so well! Thanks for asking."

"We are your psychic sisters," Tamiko said. "It's on Friday night, two weeks from now. Does that work for you?"

"Of course! The Vista Green dance is on that Saturday," I said, and then I thought of something. "Is there some rule that everyone has to buy their dresses from Glimmer?"

Tamiko snorted. "That fancy-pants place? No way. Why? And what do you mean 'everyone has to'? Says who?"

At that moment Tanner came through the door of the shop.

"I'll tell you later," I said. "Gotta go."

"Bye-eeeeeee!" Tamiko and Sierra sang, and the chat ended.

Tanner walked over to the table I was at and dumped his backpack onto one of the chairs. Mom came from behind the counter with a plate of apples and two glasses of ice water for us. "Hi, sweetie!" she said.

"Can't I have a chocolate cone?" Tanner asked.

"It's nice to see you too, Tanner," Mom teased. "And no ice cream today. We've all been overdoing it with the ice cream."

Tanner frowned. "But I'm huuuuungry."

Some more customers came in, and I knew Mom didn't have the time to deal with a cranky Tanner.

"Let's eat some apples," I said. "And then I'll help you with your homework."

Mom smiled gratefully.

Tanner frowned, but he sat down and started shoving apple slices into his mouth. I opened his backpack, looked in his homework folder, and was happy to see that he only had a vocabulary quiz coming up in a few days. Helping Tanner with vocab was a lot more fun for me than helping him with other subjects.

After we settled in, I started quizzing him. I wrote out his list of vocab words on a sheet of paper and handed it to him. I kept the paper with the definitions on it.

"All right, Tanner," I began, "which of your vocabulary words means 'thinking or listening carefully'?"

"'Attention'!" Tanner replied quickly.

"Right!" I said. "Can you use it in a sentence?"

"If I pay attention in class, Mom might give me some ice cream," Tanner said with a grin, and then he stuck his tongue out at me. I shook my head, but I didn't criticize him, because at least he'd used the word correctly.

Tanner, I was proud to notice, whizzed through the rest of his vocab words pretty smoothly, even if he did manage to work the words "ice cream" into just about every sample sentence he gave me. Then he did his math worksheet while I did some of my homework. He of course finished before I did and started playing a game on the tablet that Mom kept at the shop for him. By the time I'd finished my Italian worksheet, Rashid and Daphne had arrived and it was time for us to go.

"Call me if you need anything," Mom told them, "and thanks!"

"You got it, Meg," Rashid replied as he and Daphne reached for their aprons with the Molly's logo on them. I caught Daphne smiling at him, and I wondered if Sierra was right—if there was something to this "Raphne" thing after all. I'd have to mention it the next time Sierra and I talked.

Then Mom drove us back to our little house by the beach, and we ate a home-cooked meal of stew and biscuits. It was sort of how things used to be. Well, except Dad wasn't there.

"Can I have ice cream for dessert?" Tanner asked.

Mom sighed. "Sure, Tanner. I've got some vanilla in the fridge."

I headed into my room on the first floor. It was smaller than the room I'd had in our old house, but there was enough space for my bookshelves, and that was all that mattered, really. Plus, it made for a cozy spot for reading.

Normally with my homework done I would have curled up with a good book, but I still had the

Fall Frolic on my mind. I opened up my closet and searched until I found my nicest dress. It had a velvet top and a midnight–blue tulle skirt, with petal sleeves made of the same tulle. I had worn it the previous year, when the whole family had gotten dressed up to see the *Sleeping Beauty* ballet performed at the Green Park Opera House.

I sat down on my bed and stared at the dress in my lap. We'd gone to the ballet the previous January—not even a year before. First we'd eaten at that fancy Chinese restaurant in Green Park with the white tablecloths, and then we'd all gone to see the ballet. Mom and Dad hadn't argued at all, and Tanner had fallen asleep on Dad's arm halfway through. I had been mesmerized by the dancers, the music, and the beautiful costumes.

We'd been a complete family back then, but those days were over. I shook off a twinge of sadness, closed my bedroom door, and tried on the dress.

It still fit, although in January it had fallen half-way down my calf, and now it fell just about an inch below my knee. I knew it wouldn't work for the Vista Green dance, but I figured I could wear it to the MLK dance, maybe. I'd have to ask Sierra and Tamiko what they thought. I changed out of the dress and found Mom in the kitchen, on her laptop, frowning.

"Paying bills online might be easier, but it's still paying bills," she remarked. "What's up, Allie?"

"Well, I've got two dances coming up," I said. "There's the Fall Frolic at Vista Green, and Sierra and Tamiko got permission for me to go to the fall dance at MLK."

"Wow, that's wonderful, Allie!" she said. Then she paused. "So I guess you need a dress? What about the one you wore to the ballet?"

"I just tried it on, and it's a little short," I said. "Any chance I could get a new one?"

Mom looked down at her laptop. "I think we can afford it," she replied, and she gave me a number. "If you can stick to that budget, that is."

I hugged her. "Thanks, Mama!" I said.

I ran back into my room and went to the website for the Glimmer boutique. They had photos and prices for their dresses. I looked at the short, shimmery dresses like the one Eloise had shown me, and my mouth fell open. Each one was three times more than the budget that Mom had given me!

"No way," I said out loud, and I searched the web

for the dress shop where I had gotten the dress for the ballet. Right away I saw a bunch of dresses in my price range. I scrolled through the photos, and then stopped at a pink-and-purple dress with a scoop neck, and ruffles on the sleeves and the skirt. It looked modern and old-fashioned at the same time, and I loved it.

I found the photo on my phone and then sent it to Amanda and Eloise.

Would this work for the Vista Green dance?

Too colorful, Amanda texted back.

☹, Eloise replied. Did you look on the Glimmer site?

I sighed, went back to the Glimmer site, and scrolled through the photos. I finally found a simple silver dress with short sleeves. It just hit the knee of the model and didn't have thin straps, but I thought it might still work. The dress would show a lot more skin than I usually did, but I figured I could wear a tank top underneath or hide my bare back with my hair, just to make Mom and Dad happy. I sent a photo to Amanda and Eloise.

This one got a better response.

Cute! Amanda replied.

That could work, Eloise texted.

I sighed. It looked like I was going to have to buy the silver dress from Glimmer to fit in at the Fall Frolic. It just seemed so unfair! I mean, the silver dress was okay. I could find a way to make it work. But I didn't love it immediately the way I loved the pink and purple dress. But the last thing I needed was another excuse for the Mean Team to make comments. Plus, I'd have to come up with a lot more money on top of what Mom was giving me to buy a dress.

Where was that money going to come from? I wondered. I picked up the ceramic piggy bank next to my bed. It was bright blue with funky flowers painted on it, and it had been my mom's when she was a kid. I'd been putting my earnings from working at Molly's in it.

Well, *most* of my earnings. I knew that money had been tight for Mom since she'd opened her business, so I hadn't been bugging her for allowance and had been using my ice cream money instead. So if I went to the mall with my friends, or out for pizza or something, I paid for it myself. It was actually a pretty good feeling to be able to do that.

As I counted up the bills, quarters, dimes, and

nickels, I realized that I hadn't saved as much as I'd thought. There were two Sundays between now and the Vista Green dance. If business was really good, and people were generous with their tips, I just might make enough to buy the dress from Glimmer.

I'll have to make enough, I thought. Otherwise, I may never fit in at Vista Green!

CHAPTER THREE
CONES AND CLONES

"Rise and shine, Allie! I made pancakes!"

I slowly opened my eyes, for a second unsure where I was. Then I saw the pale blue ceiling and remembered it was Sunday morning, and I was in my room in Dad's apartment.

I yawned and looked at the clock. "It's so early!" I complained. "It's only seven thirty."

"I know, but it's supposed to be a beautiful day, and I was hoping we could go to the park before I bring you to the shop for your shift," Dad said. "And anyway, you know that Tanner still wakes up at six a.m."

"I hope he grows out of that soon," I said, sitting up. "I'll be out in a minute."

"Great, Allie. I'll keep the pancakes warm," Dad said, and he closed my bedroom door.

I climbed out of bed, and my feet hit the squishy carpet on the floor. At the beach house my bedroom had a wood floor with a cute, round rag rug right next to the bed. At Dad's the floor was carpeted. Sometimes I was hazy and confused after I woke up and didn't know where I was until my feet hit the floor.

I kept most of my stuff at Mom's house and usually brought a duffel bag with me to Dad's on the weekends when I stayed with him. Even though it had been a few months since they'd divorced, I still sometimes felt like I was staying at a hotel at Dad's house. We had to take an elevator up to the apartment; the rooms still didn't have any homey touches, just basic furniture; and I could hear people playing music and talking loudly in the apartments above us and next to us.

I put on some jeans and my Molly's T-shirt, then brushed my hair and pulled it back into a ponytail. That was how I wore it most of the time, and especially on days when I worked at Mom's shop. I had to pull it back if I was making ice cream cones, sundaes, and shakes for people all day.

Then I walked into Dad's kitchen—or was it *our* kitchen? *The* kitchen? In my head it felt like the apartment was Dad's house and the beach house was Mom's house. Before, when we'd all lived together, it had been just "our house."

Anyway, Dad had a plate of pancakes and another of bacon on the kitchen table. He and Tanner were already eating.

I sat down and yawned again—I couldn't help myself.

"So, what did you want to do at the park?" I asked Dad.

"Well, there's a nice trail there," he said. "I thought we could go for a walk. I should work off these pancakes."

Dad had started getting in better shape when he and Mom had gotten divorced. I knew it was probably because he was thinking about dating again, but I kept that thought way, way in the back of my mind.

"A walk sounds good," I said. Tamiko and Sierra were both on the softball team, and Tamiko also ran cross-country in the fall. They'd tried to get me to play softball with them, but I just wasn't interested. Sports didn't do it for me—but a nice walk in the park, well, that was just fine.

After breakfast my weather app told me it was going to be chilly until about eleven a.m., so I put on my new Vista Green hoodie—and slipped a book into the front pocket. I always had a book with me. You never knew when you'd have a chance to read.

But as it turned out, I didn't need a book that morning. Dad, Tanner, and I walked over to the Maple Grove Community Park, and we walked all the way around the trail there, past the playground, and a big fountain, and the tennis and basketball courts. Tanner ran ahead of Dad and me the whole way.

Then we went to the playground, and I could have curled up on the bench there and read, but Tanner begged me to play Shark with him. It was a game I'd made up when he was a little kid. I was the shark in the water, which was the area around the playground. All of the playground equipment was safe space. Tanner had to run around the playground and try not to be captured—and eaten, of course—by the shark.

"Dad, you be the shark," Tanner said, but my dad was on his phone.

"In a minute, Tanner," Dad said, but he had that tone of voice that meant he was busy with work, so I started to chase Tanner.

"You'd better run! I'm awfully hungry!" I said in a deep voice, and Tanner shrieked with glee as he ran away from me.

Forty-five minutes later I was panting, but it was time to head to the ice cream shop. Dad bought us hot dogs at a stand in the park, and we ate them walking back to his car.

"You know, one of these days you're going to have to feed us vegetables," I teased.

Dad laughed. "Oh, wow. You're right, Allie. Maybe tonight I'll pick us up some big salads from Pino's Pizza."

"And pizza, too. Right, Dad?" Tanner asked.

"We'll see," Dad replied. "Although, that kind of defeats the point of the salads."

"Well, if you're going to Pino's Pizza, don't you actually have to get pizza?" I asked.

"Well," Dad said sheepishly. "If that's the law."

Dad dropped me off at Mom's ice cream shop at twelve fifteen. Tamiko and Sierra didn't usually show up until twelve forty-five, but I liked to get there early to check in with Mom and get ready for the after-lunch rush. If the shop was slow, I could sneak in some rare one-on-one time with Mom then too.

It was still really weird for me to wake up and have only one parent there. I mean, there used to be some mornings when Mom or Dad would leave early for work, but I'd know that they'd both be home at night.

"Hi, Mama," I said as I went through the door.

Mom was behind the counter, and she looked pretty stressed. Her dark brown hair (the same color as mine) was falling out of the messy bun on top of her head.

She looked up at me. "Allie!" she said. "Are you having a good weekend?"

"Sure," I replied. "What about you? You look stressed."

"It's been so busy!" Mom explained. "Tamiko's idea to offer coupons to the local sports teams has been really successful—maybe too successful. I'm checking inventory now. We're totally out of Lemon Blueberry, and Chocolate Salted Caramel."

I walked over to the menu board, where the flavors were written in colorful chalk, and erased those two flavors.

"Don't worry, Mama," I said. "We've still got lots of great flavors left."

Mom sighed. "I'll have to put in extra hours this

week making ice cream," she said. "I was hoping to experiment with some new flavors, but I won't have time."

"Well, Tamiko and Sierra should be here soon," I said. "We'll take care of things up here, so you can get other stuff done."

"Paperwork!" Mom said. "It never ends!"

Mom gave me a hug. "Sorry if I sound crazy-stressed, Allie." She held me for a second. "I miss seeing you every morning." Then she took a deep breath. "Being too busy is a good problem to have when you run your own business."

"Too busy? So the new coupons are working?" Tamiko asked as she and Sierra walked through the door.

"Girls! You're here early. That's great. The coupons are fantastic," Mom replied. "Yesterday I had two girls' soccer teams in here, and a peewee football team. And the coaches all had coupons."

"Sweet, Mrs. S.!" Tamiko said. She held up her phone. "Any special flavors you want to plug today? I need to make today's FacePage post."

Mom frowned and walked up and down the counter, looking at the flavors. "I'm running out of so many! But there's a lot of Honey Pistachio. Can you plug that one for me?"

"No problemo," Tamiko replied. "Is it okay if we make a cone for the photo?"

"Knock yourself out," Mom said. "And unless you've got more questions, I'm going to go get some paperwork done and leave the shop in your capable hands."

Tamiko saluted her. "Never fear, Captain. We've got this."

I started making a Honey Pistachio ice cream cone for the photo, but I was thinking about Mom saying she missed seeing us in the morning. I missed seeing her. I missed seeing Dad, too, when he was at his house. Dad was always so excited to see us because we stayed with him less. I thought about how he must miss us too, and I felt bad. I knew they both missed us when we weren't with them. Dad seemed to have a lot of time to do . . . Well, he went to the gym a lot. And he saw a lot of movies. When we weren't there, Mom was always working at the shop or doing paperwork. She didn't have a lot of time to just chill. . . . Oops. I realized the ice cream was already starting to drip.

"How do you want to do the photo?" I asked Tamiko.

"Sierra is looking adorbs today as usual," Tamiko replied as she looked at Sierra. "What do you say, *chica*?"

Sierra shrugged. "Sure. How's my hair?"

She had pulled her curly brown hair back into a blue headband that perfectly matched the blue stripes on the chairs in the shop. She did look "adorbs," as Tamiko liked to say—but then again, Sierra always looked cute.

I handed her the cone.

"Am I supposed to be eating this? Or just looking at it?" she asked.

"Just hold it up and kind of smile at it," Tamiko said, and Sierra obliged. "Yeah, there you go. Hold on."

Tamiko snapped a few photos. "Perfect!" she said. "I've just got to post this quickly, Allie, and then I can help set up."

"No problem," I told her. "We're pretty much ready to go."

We all had different jobs at Molly's. Sierra worked the register; Tamiko took orders and made simple things, like cones; and I made the complicated orders, like shakes, mix-ins, and sundaes. But we basically all pitched in and helped make sure the napkin dispensers were filled, the tables were wiped clean, and the cookies were crushed for mix-ins—stuff like that. Tamiko was also our unofficial social media director, so she also posted when she had extra time.

"What should I do with this ice cream cone?" Sierra asked.

"Eat it!" Tamiko and I said at once, and then we both laughed.

"I will never say no to your mom's ice cream," Sierra said, and then she took a lick of the Honey Pistachio. "Mmm, that's amazing!"

Sierra finished the cone just as the after-lunch rush started. The orders came one after the other. A large cup of vanilla with crushed cookies mixed in. Two banana shakes. One strawberry sundae with vanilla ice cream and lots of strawberries. Four kiddie cones with rainbow sprinkles.

"Here's your sprinkle of happy!" I said as I helped Tamiko hand the cones to their four adorable recipients. I knew it was corny, but I loved saying it, and the customers seemed to like it too.

The stream of orders didn't stop for an hour, but I

didn't mind. When it was busy, the time went by fast. Plus, I knew that more orders usually meant more tips—which would bring me closer to buying the dress I needed for the Vista Green dance!

I was busy mixing candy into a cup of vanilla ice cream when I heard Tamiko say, "Why don't you try one of our famous mermaid cones?"

Now, a mermaid cone might sound amazing, but the problem was, we didn't have a mermaid cone on the menu. I wasn't surprised, though, because Tamiko was always making up crazy menu items to convince customers to upscale their orders. Thanks to her, we now had a dragon sundae and a unicorn sundae on the menu—so why not a mermaid cone?

I looked and saw that the woman ordering was wearing a T-shirt with a swirly mermaid design on it, which must have inspired Tamiko.

"That sounds awesome," the woman said. "What's in it?"

"Well, it's on our secret menu, so we'll have to surprise you," Tamiko replied. Then she looked at me. "One mermaid cone, Allie."

Because the customer was right there, I had to act like I knew what Tamiko was talking about. After glaring at Tamiko (but not totally meaning it, because coming up with new combinations was actually kind of fun), I stared at the ice cream flavors in the case and the toppings on the counter.

My eyes landed on the Beach Plum ice cream. A beach plum was a fruit that grew only on the East Coast. It didn't grow in Bayville, but Mom had a supplier who got it for her from Maryland. The color of the ice cream was purply-blue.

"One scoop of Beach Plum ice cream," I said, scooping it into the cone. "Plus a sprinkle of mermaid magic!"

I covered the ice cream in blue sprinkles. It wasn't super-fancy, but the mermaid fan looked pretty happy.

"Thanks," she said as I handed her the cone. "I have to post this!"

The customer took a pic of the cone with her phone. That was when I noticed Mom in the doorway, watching. She looked from me to Tamiko and then back to me again, but she was smiling.

"So that's a mermaid cone?" she asked when the customer had left.

"I thought of the concept," Tamiko said, "and Allie used her ice cream genius to make it a reality."

"You know what? I love the idea," Mom said. "It's perfect for a beachside ice cream parlor. But I think it needs a little pizzazz. I'll be right back. I'm just going to the van."

A few minutes later she returned with a small box.

"I ordered some new toppings that I wanted to experiment with," she said. "I think this will be perfect." She took out a jar of what looked like blue glitter. "*Edible* glitter," Mom said. "I think we should try mixing it into the sprinkles."

"Yes!" I cheered, and I dumped some blue sprinkles into a small plastic container. Then I took the glitter from Mom and stirred some of it into the sprinkles.

"Ooh, that's beautiful!" Tamiko said. "I have to post this, like, now. Quick, Allie, make another cone!"

I quickly made another cone, and the glitter in the blue sprinkles made all the difference. Tamiko was taking a picture of it in my hand when two girls in college sweatshirts walked in.

"What's that?" one of them asked.

"It's a mermaid cone," Tamiko said. "We're the only shop in the country that makes them. Probably the world."

"Can I get one?" the girl asked.

Tamiko took the cone from my hands. "Here you go. Should I make another one for your friend?"

The other girl nodded. If she had come in thinking of eating something else, Tamiko had made it impossible for her to order anything but a mermaid cone. Tamiko was a sales genius.

"One more mermaid cone," Tamiko said, beaming at me. She was very proud of her sales skills, and I didn't blame her.

Things slowed down for a bit, and then they got crazy. First, a bunch of girls came in, asking for mermaid cones. They had seen Tamiko's post.

Next, a group of boys in soccer uniforms came in, herded by four adults. One of the moms held up her phone and walked up to Tamiko, who was helping me make mermaid cones.

"We'd like to use the sports coupon," the woman said. "Half off cones for players, right?"

"Right!" Tamiko replied. "Just let me finish this cone, and I'll start taking your orders."

"I'll help as soon as I ring up the mermaids," Sierra offered.

"Thanks, Sierra!" I called out.

Tamiko and I handed the mermaid cones to the

customers waiting, and then the soccer kids started giving their orders. The first boy ordered a vanilla cone.

Tamiko glanced inside the ice cream case, and I guess she noticed that the vanilla was low.

"Vanilla is awesome," she said, "but what about banana? It's high in potassium and keeps your leg muscles from cramping."

"Okay!" the boy said.

"Allie, one banana cone, please!" she called out.

"Coming right up!" I called back.

The next boy wanted vanilla too, and Tamiko talked him into chocolate. As Tamiko made the chocolate cone, Sierra started taking orders.

"One vanilla cone," I heard her say. "Who else wants a vanilla cone?"

Four hands shot up right away.

"Sierra, we're almost out of vanilla!" Tamiko hissed. "I've been trying to sell the other flavors!"

"All right. Chill," Sierra replied. "How was I supposed to know?"

"I've been talking people out of vanilla all day!" Tamiko said. "Didn't you hear?"

"I've been focusing on ringing up orders," Sierra

protested. "I don't pay attention to everything that's going on at the counter."

Now, I had known Tamiko and Sierra for a long time. I knew they were very close. And I also knew that they argued a lot. Not big, screaming fights or anything. But a lot of times, they disagreed.

When this happened, I had to step in and smooth things out between them. I mean, I guess I didn't have to, but it had sort of become my job. Tamiko and Sierra bickered, and I was the peacemaker. We kind of had our roles.

"It's not a big deal," I said. "Tamiko, keep taking orders. Sierra and I will handle the vanilla. Sierra, how much vanilla is left?"

Sierra checked the bin. "I think we can get one more cone out of it."

"Okay," I said. "That cone goes to the first kid who asked for it."

I looked out at the small crowd of boys. "Now, who else wanted vanilla?"

The four boys raised their hands again.

"We're out of vanilla," I said, and a few of them groaned. I thought quickly. I knew we had an almost-full tub of Cookies and Cream in the case.

"But don't worry. We have *bonus* vanilla."

"What's bonus vanilla?" one of the boys asked.

"It's vanilla with cookies mixed in," I replied.

"Like Cookies and Cream?" he pressed.

"Yes, like Cookies and Cream," I said. "It's vanilla, but with a free helping of cookies. That's why it's called 'bonus vanilla.' So who wants a bonus vanilla cone?"

This time seven boys raised their hands.

"Great," I said. "Seven cones coming up. And who wants a sprinkle of happy?"

Fifteen minutes later the soccer team and the four parents were happily seated at our tables, eating their ice cream cones. Mom walked in and shook her head.

"This is amazing," she said. "I heard your whole 'bonus vanilla' pitch, Allie. Good thinking. You know, not many people who aren't in the ice cream business know this, but vanilla is actually the most popular ice cream flavor in the world. I have to remember to always make extra vanilla."

"Thanks, Mom," I said. "And, yes, extra vanilla would be good!"

"And, Tamiko, the sports coupon idea has brought

so much business," she said. "Thank you, too."

"It's what I do, Mrs. S.!"

Then Mom turned to Sierra. "And thank you for staying focused on the register. That's an important job, and it's easy to make mistakes. But I know you always have it under control."

Sierra smiled. "Thanks!"

We had a steady stream of customers for the last hour of our shift. At five o'clock Mom came out to work the counter, and Tamiko, Sierra, and I counted out our tips at a table in the corner.

"Sweet!" Tamiko said. "I've decided to start putting away part of my tips for my family trip to Tokyo next summer, and this is a great start."

It was definitely more tips than we'd ever received before. "I'm saving up for a dress," I told them. "If we get good tips again next week, I might just make it."

"You've got a dress picked out?" Sierra asked. "Can we see it?"

I hesitated. I had a feeling that Tamiko and Sierra wouldn't react to the dress the way that Amanda and Eloise had. But I couldn't keep the Vista Green dress a secret from them. I found the picture on my phone and showed it to them.

Tamiko raised her eyebrows. "Seriously, Ali Dali? That dress does not look like you."

"It's very . . . mature," Sierra said carefully. I knew she really didn't like it and was trying to be polite.

I could feel myself blushing a little. "I know," I said, "but I have to get a dress like this or I won't fit in at the Vista Green dance."

Tamiko and Sierra looked at each other.

"What?" I asked.

"Well, that's not surprising," Tamiko said. "It's the Vista Green Clone Syndrome."

"The *what*?" I asked.

"Nobody calls it that," Sierra told Tamiko.

"Well, *I* do," Tamiko said. "And anyway, you know what I mean. Everyone at MLK knows it. The kids at Vista Green dress like clones. The girls all have long, straight hair. They all wear the same skinny jeans. The boys all wear the same brand of cargo shorts. Everyone has the same kind of back-pack, too."

"That's not true!" I insisted. "Colin doesn't wear cargo shorts. And Amanda and Eloise don't have long straight hair."

"Well, maybe not *everybody* does," Sierra said.

"But most kids do. They're just not the kids you hang out with."

"So there is hope for you yet, Padawan," Tamiko said. I grinned at Tamiko's Star Wars reference. "Do not go to the Dark Side. Do not buy that dress."

I shut off the phone. "You really don't like the dress?" I asked.

"Don't get me wrong. It's pretty," Sierra said. "But it's just not an Allie dress."

"Plus it would make you look older, and not in a good way," Tamiko added. "And, seriously, your mom will never be okay with it."

I sighed. The nice feeling I'd gotten from the tips was slowly fading. I didn't want to be a clone. But I still wanted to fit in.

Why was getting a pretty dress for a dance turning out to be so complicated?

CHAPTER FOUR
BACK AND FORTH

Monday mornings after a Dad weekend were always pretty hectic. After Tanner and I got dressed and ate breakfast, Dad had to drive us back to Mom's house to catch the bus, or he just drove us to school. If we had time, he dropped off our overnight bags; otherwise he brought them over after work. He only lived a few minutes away from Mom, but a few extra minutes in the morning somehow threw us all off.

When Dad dropped me off at Vista Green, I found myself looking with new eyes as I scanned the stream of students heading into the building. The first thing I noticed was that everyone did have the same backpack. Every backpack I saw had the same brand name stitched onto the front pocket. They were blue, green, or purple, but they were all the same model.

As I walked to my locker, I noticed that almost every single girl had long, straight hair. I didn't see any curly hair. No short hair. And I was almost the only one wearing my hair in a ponytail.

I paid attention to legs and feet as I walked to first period. Just about every girl was wearing skinny jeans in the same shade of blue, paired with a low sneaker with a flat sole, and ankle socks that peeked out just a tiny bit from the sneakers.

Tamiko and Sierra had been right, I realized. Even though everybody had a different hair color, and eye color, and skin color, almost everyone was dressed like a clone!

I was dying to ask my new friends about it at lunchtime, but I knew I had to approach it in just the right way.

"So, um, remember how you guys were saying that everyone has to get the same kind of dress for the Fall Frolic?" I asked Eloise and Amanda.

"Uh-huh." Amanda nodded as she ate her sandwich.

"Well, does that go for every day at Vista Green too?" I asked. "I mean, you know how a lot of girls have the same hair and the same style of jeans? And the way the boys wear cargo shorts?"

"Yeah, it's the Clone Syndrome," Eloise replied.

"That's what my friend Tamiko called it! But I thought she'd just made that up," I said.

Amanda shrugged. "Well, I think it's one of those things that everybody knows about but nobody really talks about," she said. "It started back in fifth grade, I think. All of a sudden, everyone was letting their hair grow long, and straightening it if it was curly. Which is a lot easier for some people to do than others, so I just do my hair the way I like it."

"Me too," Eloise replied, twirling a finger around one of her blond curls. "Chemical hair straightening is so expensive, and it's bad for your hair, and I am not going to get up an hour earlier just to straighten my hair with a flat iron."

"It's probably one reason why Eloise and I will never be popular," Amanda said with a laugh. "Which is fine, because we don't care about being popular."

"Me neither," I replied. "But I'm a little confused. Why do you still think we need to wear short dresses with spaghetti straps from Glimmer to the dance?"

"Well, the dance is different," Amanda explained.

"It's a big deal, and you don't want to stand out for the wrong reasons, you know?"

"I guess," I said with a frown, and then I ate my lunch, thinking.

When the bell rang, Colin walked with me to my math class.

"I heard you guys talking about the Clone Syndrome," he said with a smile.

I shook my head. "I still can't believe that's a thing."

"Don't worry, Allie. You're not a clone. That's why I like you," he said, and then he started to blush. "I mean, why we *all* like you. Me and Amanda and Eloise."

I felt myself blushing too. Had Colin just said that he liked me? And did he mean that he liked me, or that he *liked* me? The thought made me feel happy and a little freaked out at the same time.

Luckily, I spent the next forty-five minutes in math class learning how to calculate ratios and didn't have any brain space left to think about clones or dresses or cute boys who might like me.

After school I walked over to Molly's and found Mom spraying and wiping the tables.

"Here, let me do that," I offered.

"Oh, thank you, Allie," Mom said, and I noticed she looked a little paler than usual and that she had bags under her eyes.

"You look tired," I said.

She nodded. "I stayed up late last night trying to make some new batches of ice cream because we ran out of so much this weekend," she said. "I still need to catch up, so Dad's going to pick up you and Tanner today so that I can make ice cream after the shop closes."

"Tonight?" I asked, and I realized I was disappointed. The beach house felt more like home than Dad's apartment, and I hadn't slept there since Thursday. "But we don't have any extra clothes packed. And I was hoping to do laundry so that I could wear my blue shirt tomorrow, the one with the flowers on the collar. It's such a pain to do laundry in Dad's building because I have to go to the basement to use the washing machine!"

Mom sighed. "It's just for tonight, Allie. I promise. Dad will take you to the house after he picks you up here, and you can pack a fresh bag for you and Tanner," she said. "This will really help me get back on track, sweetie. And it's nice of your dad to be so flexible with the visitation."

Visitation. I hated that word. It was a term that

people used when they were in jail or the hospital. It didn't feel like the right word to use to describe me and Tanner spending time with our own father.

"Fine, Mom!" I said, trying to sound cheerful. I knew that Mom was going through a lot, with the divorce and the new business, and she needed lots of encouragement. The last thing she needed was for me to be in a bad mood and add to her problems. But I was still mad. I didn't like not knowing which house I'd be in each night. It was like my parents were playing a game of tag.

Mom smiled and gave me a kiss. "I will make it up to you, Allie," she said. "Besides, Dad misses you too, and he was so excited to be able to see you and Tanner again tonight. He says the apartment is too quiet without you!"

Now, while Mom was stressed out and always working, Dad, on the other hand, seemed to be doing just fine since the divorce. He loved living in the apartment, and his job was the same as always. Sure, he might say he didn't like the quiet, but I was a little skeptical about that. So I usually saved up all of my complaining for him. He came to the shop at five, while I was helping Tanner with his homework, as usual.

"Are you guys ready for another Dad night?" he asked as we piled into the car.

"Yay!" Tanner cheered.

"Not really," I said. "I was hoping to do some laundry at the house tonight. And Diana must really be missing us."

Diana was our family cat. Mom had gotten custody of her, which was fine, but it also stank that I didn't get to see her every day anymore.

"It's just for tonight, Allie," Dad said, repeating Mom's words. "And it will really help your mom. Plus, I really like having you guys for an extra night."

"Yeah, I heard," I mumbled.

He pulled up in front of the beach house.

"I'll get a bag for me *and* Tanner," I said loudly, emphasizing the "and" to show Dad what a pain it was for me to have to do it. And I might have stomped my feet a little bit on the walk to the front door.

Diana ran up to me as soon as I walked in, and wove between my ankles, purring. I picked her up and kissed the top of her head.

"Sorry, girl," I said. "We can't hang out until tomorrow. Unless, of course, Mom and Dad change the schedule again."

Then I put her down, fed her (as Mom had asked me to), dumped out the dirty clothes in my duffel bag and Tanner's, and then packed clean clothes for us both. The only pair of jeans in my drawer were a pair of blue skinny jeans, and I shook my head as I shoved them into my bag. I didn't wear them often, but I had no other choice.

Clone for a day, I thought.

My phone buzzed with a text from Sierra in our group chat.

How do you feel about this dress? Sierra had attached a picture of herself in a light, flowing dress that almost reached her ankles. It was white and covered with bright colorful flowers.

Is it for the MLK dance? I texted back. It's cute!

Mm-hmm! I found it in my cousin's closet. I might borrow it.

A few moments later Tamiko responded. It's totally off-season. Perfect for a spring wedding but not for a fall dance.

Tamiko had a point—she was the fashion expert, after all. The dress was pretty, but it didn't feel autumn-y.

Dances are always so warm, though, Sierra

responded. Cuz there are so many people and you're moving around.

Fashion over function! Tamiko shot back. Also, the colors of the flowers would clash with the decorations, right? Wouldn't you know, since you're on the committee?

I get it. Jeez! I'll find another dress.

Sierra sounded annoyed, so I felt like I needed to respond and keep the peace . . . like always. But before I could type a response, Tanner was yelling from the front door for me to hurry up. I grabbed the two duffel bags and rushed out.

Dad took me and Tanner out for dinner at the Bayville Diner. Dad liked it there because they played his kind of music, classic rock, over the speakers, and he said that they had the best hamburgers in the area. Dad didn't cook a lot. He could grill, but he didn't have a grill in his new apartment and didn't usually have much cooking stuff in his kitchen, so we went out a lot when we were with him. I got a tuna melt and fries, my usual order, and Tanner got the meat loaf platter with mashed potatoes. When the food arrived, he started shoveling chunks of meat loaf dipped in potatoes into his mouth.

"Tanner, slow down!" I said.

"I'm hungry!" he objected with his mouth full of food. "Today, in gym, we played touch football outside, and everybody made me captain and I ran all the way down the field and made a touchdown and nobody could touch me because I am so fast and all that running made me hungry!"

"Good job, buddy," Dad said.

I put down a french fry and stared at Tanner. "They made you captain?" I asked, knowing that only popular kids get picked to be captain in gym class.

Tanner nodded and shoved another forkful of food into his mouth. "I'm the best at football. José and Carter and Brayden all say so."

"Are those your friends?" I asked him.

"My best friends," Tanner replied.

"Your best friends?" I asked. "What about George and Mason from your old school?"

Tanner shrugged. "I got new ones," he said. "Carter is awesome. The other day in class he burped, and everyone was laughing, even Mrs. Young, because he said he couldn't help himself, and it was awesome, the loudest burp you've ever heard."

"He sounds like a real winner," I said.

"You've made some friends in your new school, haven't you, Allie?" Dad asked. "Those girls you were telling me about? Mindy . . . and Elyse?"

"You mean *Amanda*, who lives in your building, not 'Mindy,'" I corrected him. "And *Eloise*, not 'Elyse.'"

"Sorry, hon. I'm so bad with names," Dad said. "But it's nice that you have friends too."

"They're nice, and I'll probably go to Fall Frolic with them," I said. "Still, it's not the same as Tamiko and Sierra."

"Fall Frolic?" Dad repeated. "What's that?"

"Didn't I tell you about the school dance that's happening in two weeks?" I asked, trying not to sound exasperated. Dad frowned and shook his head.

It was so confusing to keep track of what I told Mom and what I told Dad. It was much easier when we used to live in the same house and we just all talked at dinner.

Tanner kept on chatting with his mouth full about José and Carter and Brayden, and while I was totally disgusted with his eating habits, I couldn't help admiring his happy school life. He had traded in his

54

old best friends for new ones easily and seemed to have become instantly popular.

I sighed. I couldn't go to my old school anymore, and I still didn't feel like I belonged at my new school. I got to spend time with Dad, or Mom, but not Dad and Mom together. And even though I lived in two different places, neither of them felt like home yet. I was stuck in some weird middle ground.

I picked up my tuna melt. I liked the ones they made in Bayville because they made them on rye bread, and not open-faced on English muffins like over at the Gold Star Diner. As I raised the sandwich to my lips, the word "sandwich" echoed in my head.

Sandwiched. That was what I was. Stuck between two worlds, just like the tuna and mushed cheese inside my bread.

CHAPTER FIVE
WORLDS APART

Although I was sure that nothing would ever make up for my not being in the same school as Tamiko and Sierra, there were a few things about Vista Green that I liked a lot.

One of them was the school library, which had three times as many books as the MLK library, and opened up to a garden outside, where you could eat lunch in the nice weather. Inside, you could sit on a comfy couch and read, or sit in one of the beanbag chairs. The librarian, Mrs. K., was a little prickly, but in kind of a hedgehog way—not scary at all; she'd been nice to me since my first day of school. I liked the library so much that for the first few weeks of school, I had spent every lunch period there, until

Amanda had convinced me that I should sit with her and Colin and Eloise. But I still spent at least one lunch a week down there, and sometimes I helped out Mrs. K. after school.

Another great thing about Vista Green was Ms. Healy, my English teacher. She was really enthusiastic and fun to be around, and her classroom was like a perfect laboratory for creativity. There were beanbag chairs in there, too, along with more shelves filled with books, and stacks of blank paper and jars of colorful markers that we could use whenever we were inspired. My favorite thing about the room was the border of the classroom at the top of the wall, where Ms. Healy had hung portraits of famous writers with their names underneath. The border went all the way around the room.

And every single day Ms. Healy started the class with a "disco minute," to get our creative juices flowing. That Tuesday was no different. We all danced around to blaring pop music underneath the swirling lights of a disco ball for sixty seconds, and then the music and lights stopped.

"We're all going to need to tap into our creativity today," Ms. Healy began. "Today we're going to learn about a form of poetry called a haiku. We'll practice writing one, and then work on perfecting the haiku for homework. Now, does anybody know what a haiku is?"

A few hands shot up, including mine. Ms. Healy called on Colin.

"It's a form of Japanese poetry, with three lines," he replied.

Ms. Healy nodded. "That's right. And each line has a specific amount of syllables. The first line has five syllables, the second line has seven, and the third line has five."

She pressed some keys on her laptop, and a haiku appeared on the white wall behind her desk.

"Here's one I wrote when I took my walk this morning," she said.

A seagull swoops down
Picks up a fish in her beak
Now I want breakfast

We all laughed.

"So, what do you notice about this haiku, besides the syllables?" Ms. Healy asked.

"It's funny," a boy named Aaron said.

"I'm glad you think so," Ms. Healy said. "Anything else?"

"Well, it lets you form a picture in your mind," said Maria. She was one of the Mean Team; although, of the three of them, she was probably the nicest. "Like, I could picture the seagull swooping down and getting the fish."

I raised my hand. "The last line was sort of surprising," I said. "I wasn't expecting the poem to end up that way."

Ms. Healy nodded. "That's a good observation, Allie," she said. "The syllable rules of a haiku might seem restrictive, but you can have fun playing with the format. Think about how the three lines can relate to one another."

Suddenly I was itching to write a haiku.

"I'm going to give everyone twenty minutes to play around with the haiku form in your journals," she went on. "You can upload them onto my homework page tonight. Write about whatever you want. Your haiku can be about something small, like breakfast, or about something more important in your life."

Then she typed on her keyboard again, and some

soft classical music played from the speakers on her desk. Ms. Healy believed that the right music could "free your thoughts."

I opened my journal and stared at the blank page, thinking. There had been so many changes in my life lately; it only seemed natural to write about them. First I thought about not being in school with Tamiko and Sierra anymore. I started to write, playing around with the lines as I counted the syllables.

> *My best friends are ~~in another school~~ far*
> *I miss them ~~a lot every day~~ all of the time*
> *~~Everything is different~~ Nothing is the same*

I liked it, but it was kind of depressing. I thought about the ice cream shop—that was one of the happy changes that had happened. I looked up at Ms. Healy's haiku on the wall, and the word "swoops" made me think of the word "scooping." Suddenly the poem came to me.

> *Scooping out ice cream*
> *Hoping it is a big hit*
> *Making my mom proud*

I liked that haiku, but then thinking about the ice cream shop reminded me of the whole reason why it existed—because Mom and Dad had divorced.

> *Feeling so ~~sad~~ alone*
> *My mom and dad are ~~separated divorced~~ apart*
> *I am so confused*

It was another depressing haiku, but I figured that was all right. Although, I thought maybe the third line could use some work. But Ms. Healy said it was time for us to move on, and I vowed to make some improvements on it that night.

After school that day I didn't go straight to the ice cream shop. Instead I texted Mom, then stopped at the beach house, got my bike, and rode it over to the library. It was farther away from the beach house than from our old house, but the route was a little safer because there was a bike lane for most of it. Two hours a week I volunteered in the tutoring program at the library, where I helped kids with reading.

Sometimes I just read to them to help them get into a book, and other times I let them practice their reading skills on me while the adult teacher who ran the program helped other kids. My favorite part was connecting the kids with books that were either my own favorites or just right for them. It made me so happy when one of the kids came running in with a book we'd picked together the previous week, and said, *Allie! Allie! You were right! I loved it!*

Many of the kids in the program were new immigrants to the United States. Sometimes their parents didn't speak any English, but it made me happy to see how quickly the children learned to use the library. And if you're feeling sad or a little alone, there's nothing better than getting lost in a good book.

At the library I said hi to the other volunteer I knew, and the teacher, and then gathered kids in the program. There was a new kid today about my age, a petite, pretty girl with dark eyes that were like huge brown pools. She looked super-nervous, and she kept fidgeting with her head scarf. I smiled and waved at her, and a flicker of friendliness crossed her face, but she still looked a little cautious. I wondered where she was from and what she had gone through to get here.

"Hi," I said softly. "I'm Allie."

She smiled tentatively and touched her chest. "Noor."

"Do you like to read?" I asked. I gestured at the books spread out on a low table. I couldn't tell how good her English was, but she seemed to understand me. She nodded.

"Should we read?" I said.

Again she nodded, so we sat.

I gestured to all the books and asked her to pick one. To my surprise, she picked one that was probably the highest reading level. I started to take it from her so that I could read it to her, but she smiled and shook her head. She opened the book and began to read, perfectly.

I was so impressed. It was a book about horses and girls riding over the countryside in Virginia. I studied Noor, wondering how old she was. She was very small and could have been a fourth grader, but poise-and-maturity-wise she might have been an eighth grader. As she read on, it was clear that she understood everything that was happening in the book. When she had finished the chapter, she placed the book down on the table and smiled at me shyly.

"Wow, Noor! That was great!" I said. "Where did you learn English?"

"I am from Iraq. An American lady set up a school

for girls, and we all learned reading and writing. Then we learned English." Noor's eyes shone with pride.

"How old are you?" I asked.

"Eleven," she said. "I am in sixth grade at Martin Luther King Middle School."

"I used to go there! But now I'm at Vista Green." We smiled at each other. "I love to read," I said.

"Me too," Noor said. "Right now I am reading the Secret Sisters series."

"That's a great series!" I said.

"I am waiting to read the latest book, but the library does not have it yet," Noor said. "I am very anxious to find out if Erin will find the hidden room in the old house."

"I don't mean to be rude, but why do you need tutoring?" I asked.

"I am always wanting to get better. Also, I brought my little brother today. He is not so good as I am, even though I try to teach him."

I rolled my eyes. "Little brothers are the worst!"

She laughed and agreed. "My best friend back home also had a little brother," she said. "He and Zayid used to get into so much trouble always."

"Do you miss your friends back home?" I asked.

Noor nodded, and she looked a little sad. "I do," she said, "but I hope to make some new ones." She gave me a hopeful smile, and I smiled back. "Besides," she said, "sometimes change is good. It gives you new opportunities."

I thought about that for a second. Change lately had been pretty bad, if you asked me. Maybe it was working out better for her.

"Well, I don't think you need me to help tutor you," I said. "But maybe you could help me tutor some of the younger kids?"

She nodded. "I'd like that."

"Great! Let's go over there and see who we can help," I said, and we crossed the room to the gaggle of kids in the picture book area. I was happy to have found another book lover. On my ride home I wondered if Noor felt the same way I did about leaving friends and making new ones. It must have been harder for her since her friends were an ocean away. Even though Sierra and Tamiko and Dad were still close by, it felt sometimes like there was an ocean between all of them and the beach house.

That night, back at Mom's house, I put a load of laundry into the washer and then settled down to do homework. I stared at the three haikus in my journal and tried to decide which ones to send to Ms. Healy. I typed the first one into my laptop.

> *My best friends are far*
> *I miss them all of the time*
> *Nothing is the same*

I still liked my haiku, I decided, but I knew that Tamiko would say I was being a little dramatic. "We're still right here!" I could imagine her saying. A haiku popped into my head, and I sent it to them both in a group text.

> *Sunday Sundae girls*
> *Nothing can separate us*
> *Best friends forever!*

Tamiko responded right away with a big red ♥. I waited for a response from Sierra, but I didn't get one. I wondered if they were together and Tamiko had responded for both of them.

Are you with Sierra? I texted Tamiko.

No, she responded. A few seconds later she added,

She's probs too busy signing up for 500 more clubs and then regretting it.

I was surprised by Tamiko's snarky response, but I was a little annoyed at Sierra too. I tried to shake off the feeling. I knew that Sierra was probably busy with one of her many commitments, but still, when a friend sends you a sappy haiku, it deserves some kind of response, doesn't it?

Just then Tanner banged on my door. "We gotta call Dad!" he said. When we were at Dad's house, we called Mom to say good night. When we were at Mom's house, we called Dad. I got out my phone, and in about two seconds Dad's face appeared, like he had been waiting for us. After a few minutes of talking about the rest of the week, Tanner ducked out to brush his teeth. "Any big plans tonight, Dad?" I asked.

He laughed and panned the phone around so that I could see the empty apartment. "Pretty quiet here," Dad said. "Too quiet without you two!" I thought I heard a little bit of sadness in his voice. The apartment did seem very, very still. I had just assumed that he liked all that quiet, but maybe he really did miss us too.

I blew him a kiss, ended the call, and took the

phone downstairs, since Mom didn't let me keep the phone in my room at night. I thought about the empty apartment and imagined Dad wandering around. I thought about Sierra out doing something and me not knowing what. Why, I wondered, couldn't everything be the nice, familiar way it used to be? Change might have been working for Noor, but it was definitely not working for me.

CHAPTER SIX
POETRY, SLAMMED

Sierra finally did answer my text the next day, with a poem of her own.

> *Roses are red,*
> *Violets are blue.*
> *I love my friends,*
> *And they love me too!*

That made me laugh, and I forgave her for not getting back to me right away.

But as soon as the bus arrived at school, the fuzzy feeling faded. I looked out into the sea of straight hair, skinny jeans, and backpacks. This time I noticed that a lot of the girls were wearing fur-lined boots that almost looked like bed slippers. Some girls wore light brown boots, while others wore dark brown boots, but they were clearly all the same style. It was bizarre that everyone was wearing furry boots, since the weather outside was beautiful. I hadn't even brought a sweater to school. Maybe the boots were meant to be "in season" regardless of weather. I wished I could ask Tamiko about it.

Since I had had the realization that I was going to school among clones, I had been feeling kind of weird. So that day at lunch I decided to duck into the library and get lost in the book I was currently reading.

When I walked in, Mrs. K. was seated at her desk. She looked up at me through the funky rectangular glasses perched on her nose. She was the most color-ful librarian I'd ever met, and today she had on a silky orange blouse and a necklace of chunky sapphire-blue and silver beads.

"Good afternoon, Allie. Did you come here to read, or can you shelve some books for me?" she asked.

"Can I shelve after I finish my sandwich?" I asked.

"Yes, you may," she replied. "Sandwich, then

shelve. But please be sure to wash your hands first. We must not get the books dirty."

The way Mrs. K. spoke, you might not think she was a friendly person. That was just how she was. She always got to the point pretty quickly. But she was also very nice. She had never once said anything about me spending my lunch period in the library. It was like she knew I was looking for a safe spot to hide out, and she always welcomed me in.

I was stacking books (with clean hands) when she walked up to me.

"I see that Ms. Healy is beginning her poetry unit," she said. "What do you think of that?'"

I realized that I hadn't formed an opinion about it until she asked me. "Well, I like poetry just fine, I guess," I said. "But it's not the same to me as getting lost in a story in a book."

"That is how most people think, I fear," she said. "But I don't think you can compare poetry and fiction. The great poet E. E. Cummings famously said that poetry was the only thing that mattered. But he was a poet, so he had a good reason to say that."

"We haven't really started reading a lot of poems yet," I said. "Maybe I just need to connect with a poet the way I connect with my favorite writers."

"You are in good hands with Ms. Healy," Mrs. K. said. "She has turned many students into poetry lovers."

I didn't think about poetry at all while I was calculating ratios, but in Ms. Healy's class, after our disco minute, she made an announcement.

"I have read through your haikus," she said. "You guys did a great job. I saw a lot of creativity and sensitivity in your poems."

"Yeah, I'm so sensitive!" Sean Smith blurted out, and everyone cracked up, I guess because Sean was the class clown. He wasn't mean, but he teased people a lot and never seemed to take anything too seriously.

"I'm thinking that at the end of this unit, we can have a poetry slam," Ms. Healy went on, "where everybody who wants to can read their poetry out loud. But for today I'm going to read your haikus anonymously. If you don't want to admit to being the author, you don't have to. All right. Let's begin."

She started off reading a sweet haiku about a kitten:

"I love my kitten
He likes to play with his toys
And that makes me smile!"

Nobody said it was theirs, although I did notice that Jasmine Day's face turned bright red when Ms. Healy was reading. Then Ms. Healy read a funny haiku about pizza.

"Pizza is the best.
A cheesy delight, oh boy!
Food, glorious food!"

Everybody laughed. "That's mine!" John Carboni announced.

"That figures," Sean said. "You should see this boy eat!"

"All right, settle down, Sean," Ms. Healy said. "The next haiku is especially strong.

"Reporting events
Pitching column ideas
Newspaper is great!

"Do you notice that the poet uses the first two lines to describe something, but waits until the last line to reveal what is being described? This technique keeps the reader engaged until the end of the poem, because they want to know what the poem is about!"

"That's my poem," Colin said, beaming. I caught myself grinning, even though Ms. Healy's compliment hadn't been directed at me.

"This next poet submitted two haikus," Ms. Healy continued. "Here's the first one.

"My best friends are far . . ."

Hearing Ms. Healy read my haiku out loud made me want to sink into the floor! The words sounded so cheesy! And so personal!

Don't worry, I told myself. *Nobody has to know that you wrote it!*

But then Ms. Healy started to read the second poem I had submitted.

"Scooping out ice cream . . ."

74

My stomach sank. I knew I was doomed. And as soon as Ms. Healy finished, I heard Blair (the queen mean girl) snicker behind me.

"Ooh, I wonder who that can be?" she said, and a few kids laughed. Then Blair tapped me on the shoulder. "You're writing poems about scooping ice cream? About your job in your mommy's shop? Get a life!"

I could feel my face burning. Out of the corner of my eye, I saw Colin give me a sympathetic look, but it only made me feel worse somehow.

"Blair, I'd like to remind you of our class covenant," Ms. Healy said. "We treat one another with respect and kindness in this room." She looked around the room. "And let me remind you all that poetry, like all art forms, is subjective. You might think a poem isn't so great, while somebody else thinks it's the best poem in the world. So as part of this unit, we're going to learn about constructive criticism. That means when we comment on somebody's work, we're going to keep our comments helpful, whether you like what you've read or not. So, Blair, do you want to rephrase that comment?"

"Well, Allie, I think I would like your poem better if it wasn't about your du—your boring job," Blair said. A few people snickered.

Ms. Healy frowned at Blair. I felt even more mortified, now that everybody was making a big deal out of it. Ms. Healy started to say something more, but then she saw how red my face was turning and decided not to. I said a little thank-you to Ms. Healy in my heart.

"On to the next haiku," Ms. Healy said, and she read it out loud.

"I love my thick hair!
It is shiny and perfect.
My crowning glory."

"I wrote that," Blair announced proudly.

"Wait. . . . Blair, did you actually write a poem about your *hair?*" Sean asked. "Seriously?"

A few kids laughed, and I felt totally relieved. "Oh," said Sean in a high voice, "it's just perfect." And then he flipped his head. Everyone roared. For once, one of Blair's comments had backfired on her!

Ms. Healy sighed. "I think we need a short lesson

76

in constructive criticism before we can continue," she said. "Let's all take a deep breath and think about how powerful words are, if we use them in a poem or we use them in everyday language. They should be used with care."

Poetry *was* powerful, I realized, thinking about all of the drama that had ensued in class because of just a few haikus. I tried to imagine what a class poetry slam would be like, and the thought made me nervous. I already knew what it felt like to have my poetry slammed by Blair. I wasn't sure that I wanted that to happen again!

CHAPTER SEVEN
#SAVETHECOOKIES

"No way! Alyssa should not have told Rachel what Victoria said," Sierra was saying as she and Tamiko walked into the ice cream shop on Sunday.

"Of course she should have!" Tamiko argued. "Rachel deserved to know, and she and Victoria are friends. Victoria never should have told Alyssa if she didn't want Rachel to know."

I felt a little ignored. I'd kind of been expecting a big, happy reunion since we'd been apart since the previous Sunday.

I cleared my throat loudly. "Uh, hello? Best friend here. You know, the one you haven't seen in a whole week?"

"Sorry, Ali Sally," Tamiko said, and she ran behind

the counter to give me a huge crazy hug. "Drama club drama. Sierra was just telling me how her friend Victoria from the drama club was mightily wronged, but I had to disagree."

"She *was* wronged," Sierra said with a heavy sigh. "And hi, Allie. Missed you!"

"I missed you too," I said. "Both of you. And I miss hearing all the MLK gossip. Are you talking about Victoria Shapiro?"

Sierra nodded. "Yes," she said. "She told Alyssa that Rachel didn't have the right singing voice for the part she got in the musical, and then Alyssa told Rachel, and now Rachel isn't speaking to Victoria and it's a huge mess."

"Hmm," I said. "Everyone knows that Alyssa and Rachel are friends, right? So Victoria was probably hoping that Alyssa would tell Rachel."

"That's exactly what I said!" Tamiko yelled.

"But still, Alyssa shouldn't have told Rachel," Sierra argued.

"Listen, if Victoria told you something bad about Tamiko, you'd tell Tamiko, right?" I asked Sierra.

Sierra nodded. "Yeah, I guess you're right. Alyssa did the right thing, I guess."

"Which is what I've been saying all along," Tamiko said to Sierra. "But you didn't agree with me."

"That's because Allie knows the right way to say things," Sierra said, giving me a smile.

Tamiko rolled her eyes,. "Yes, yes, Allie is always the peacemaker." Just then a dad-aged man walked into the store.

"Excuse me," he said. "Can I speak to the manager, please?"

"Sure," I said. "I'll get her."

"Uh-oh," Tamiko murmured as I walked past her. "We're in trouble."

I fetched Mom from the back room, and my stomach was doing flip-flops. I hoped it was nothing bad.

"Can I help you?" Mom asked, wiping her hands on her apron.

Tamiko's comment had made me a little nervous. I stared at the man, trying to remember him. Had I given him the wrong order? Had I been busy and not been friendly to him when he'd placed his order? But his face didn't ring any bells—I didn't recognize him at all.

"Yes, well. My daughter is turning nine next week, and I was wondering if we could host her birthday party here," he said. "That is, if you do that kind of thing."

I let out a big breath.

Mom looked around and smiled. "I don't see why not," she replied. "What day and time were you thinking? I'm not sure if we could do it on weekends, because we're so busy, but after school would be ideal."

"That would be perfect," the man said. "I was hoping for a Thursday afternoon. I brought my daughter in here once for some ice cream, and she said it was the best she'd ever had. She said she dreams about it!"

"Now, that's the kind of customer I love hearing about," Mom said, beaming. "I can't wait to host her party here!"

Mom took some information down while Tamiko, Sierra, and I got the shop ready for the Sunday rush.

"Please call me if you have any questions," she said, handing him her card. "We can't wait for the big day!"

"Thank you!" said the man. Mom gave him a scoop of ice cream to take with him too, and joked that he should eat it before he got home and his daughter saw it.

Mom looked really pleased after he left.

Tamiko ran up to her. "Birthday parties, Mrs. S.! This is genius!" she cried. "I can't believe I didn't think of it. We should start marketing this right away. Flyers, maybe? Or an e-mail campaign—"

"Let's hold off, Tamiko, until we see how this one goes," Mom said. "I still have to price things out. I'll need extra help for the party, and party favors, and decorations . . ."

"I can help with that, Mama," I said. "I can help you look for stuff online, and I'll work the party for free for you. And when this party is a success, Tamiko can start marketing."

Mom let out a long breath. "Thanks, Allie. I could sure use the help," she said. "And expanding is good, right? I shouldn't be afraid of expanding. That's good for business."

She sounded like she was trying to convince herself.

"Of course it is, Mrs. S.!" Tamiko said. "Don't worry. We'll have your back as you propel Molly's Ice Cream to fame and fortune. And we can help at the party too."

"For today I'll just settle for enough customers to pay the rent," Mom said.

"You know, I have an idea," Sierra piped up. "I'm on the dance committee, and I'm in charge of getting food. We have a budget and everything. What if you catered ice cream for the dance?"

"Ooh, I like that idea," Mom said. "Since it's a school event, I could do it at a discount."

"Now you're thinking like a marketer, Mrs. S.," Tamiko said. "This will be great advertising for the ice cream shop. Once people try your flavors, they'll be hooked! Plus you can come to the dance!"

Sierra looked at me to see if I minded having Mom at the dance. I thought about going back to MLK and wondered if anyone besides Sierra and Tamiko would remember me. Maybe it wouldn't be so bad to have Mom there. I gave a little nod to Sierra.

"I should make some fun fall flavors," Mom said. "Sierra, come talk to me about the number of kids going and the budget you have. It's not busy out here."

"Sure," Sierra said, and she and my mom walked to the back room, leaving me and Tamiko in the front.

Mom was right—it wasn't busy at all.

"I hope we get some customers." I sighed. "I was counting on some big tips today to buy that dress for the dance."

"Ugh! I still think you are wrong about that dress," Tamiko said. "But I'm always happy to support shopping."

"All right. Maybe we shouldn't think about customers," I said. "Maybe we're jinxing it. I'm going to cut up strawberries for the mix-ins, and then the customers will just start pouring in."

"Right!" Tamiko said. "I'll crush up some cookies."

Sierra came back into the front of the store. "I'm back at my station," she announced. "No customers yet?"

"Shhh, don't jinx it," Tamiko said. "They'll come."

The store felt a little lonely without anyone there. Although it could become hectic, I liked hearing the chatter of customers, the jingle of the door as people walked in and out, and Sierra's humming as she worked at the register. Sierra had a habit of humming whenever she was really busy—which was most of the time. But right now she just stood in front of the register, silent, waiting for something to do. I guessed that was what Dad's apartment must feel like when we weren't there. And Mom's house. The shop felt empty, and weird.

The bell on the door jingled, and we all jumped to attention as a teenage boy walked in.

"Uh, hi. Can I have a chocolate shake?" he asked.

"Sure. You want a large, right? You definitely need a large," Tamiko said.

"Uh, sure," he replied.

"Maybe you should get *two* shakes," Tamiko said, "in case you go home and finish this shake and you're like, 'Man, that was so good. I wish I had another one.'"

"Uh, one is fine," he said.

By that time I had his shake whirring in the machine. I handed it to him as he paid Sierra at the register and dropped two coins into the tip jar.

When he left, Tamiko ran over to the tip jar. "Fifty cents! We're rolling in it!" she joked.

"Business will pick up," Sierra said. "It always does."

"Well, until then I will crush cookies," Tamiko said.

She walked over to the cookie-crushing station behind the counter. My mom had baked some chocolate chip cookies that morning, and Tamiko's job was to crush them with a rolling pin so that I could blend them into mix-ins when people ordered them.

Tamiko picked up the rolling pin and then stopped and sighed. "These cookies are so beautiful! It is breaking my heart to crush them up!" she said. "I can't do it!"

She put down the rolling pin and picked up her phone. "Hashtag save the cookies," she said as she snapped a photo.

I laughed. "Tamiko, I know they're beautiful, but people like them in the mix-ins," I said. "Otherwise, why would you have cookies in an ice cream shop?"

"Well, you can make ice cream sandwiches out of them, can't you?" Sierra asked. "I love ice cream sandwiches! Ooey, gooey outside and cool, creamy inside!"

I stopped slicing strawberries. "Sierra, that's brilliant!"

Tamiko ran to the counter and picked up a scoop. "Let's try one with classic vanilla," she said.

"Not too much ice cream," I said. "It has to fit."

Tamiko gently put a scoop of ice cream on top of a cookie, and I topped it with another cookie, squishing it down a little bit.

"It looks good," I said. "But it needs a sprinkle of happy!"

I rolled the ice cream edges of the sandwich in the bin of chocolate sprinkles.

"That is picture-perfect!" Tamiko said. "Hold it up!"

I obeyed, and Tamiko took a picture.

"Are you posting this?" I asked.

"Yes," Tamiko said. "But I am also sending it to Kai. He has a business club meeting today, and I'm telling him he needs to bring everyone here to support a local business and take advantage of an amazing ice cream sandwich special."

The bell on the front door jingled, and a mom pushing a stroller came in. She had a baby in the stroller and a toddler holding her free hand.

"I'll have a small vanilla cone for the big brother here," she said.

"Sure," Tamiko said. "Or you could try our ice cream sandwich special today, made with freshly baked cookies. Only one dollar more than a cone, and a lot less messy!"

I held up the sample ice cream sandwich.

"Less messy sounds nice," the mom said. "Okay, I'll have one. Actually, make that two."

Some teenage girls came in next, and they all wanted mermaid cones. Mom had told me that she'd been getting orders for them all week and had needed to order more blue glitter. But we still had some. I finished with the ice cream sandwiches and made three mermaid cones.

It seemed like we had a steady stream of customers after that. And then, when we were really crowded, Kai came in with, like, twelve high schoolers!

Kai was a sophomore in high school, and he was pretty popular. Tamiko said that all of the girls thought he was cute. He might have been cute, but he was still Tamiko's brother, so we kind of didn't think of him in that way. He did have pretty awesome wavy hair, though.

"I spearheaded the social media initiative for this shop," Kai was telling the other kids. "They didn't even have a web page at launch!"

"And I am the unofficial social media director," Tamiko said, interrupting Kai.

"Yo, that's your sister, right?" one of the high school guys asked.

"That's right," Kai said. "I taught her everything she knows about marketing."

Tamiko looked like she was about to snap back at Kai, but he gave her a look—a look that said, *I can walk out of here with all twelve of these customers at any time.*

"He sure did," Tamiko said, smiling sweetly. "Now, can I get each of you an ice cream sandwich special?"

I happily lined up twenty-four cookies and started making ice cream sandwiches. It was turning out to be an awesomely busy day!

By the time our shift ended, we had sold out of cookies, and I knew I had made at least a dozen mermaid cones. And more regular cones, cups, and shakes than I could count.

Mom came out as Sierra was carefully dividing the tips.

"Mrs. S., you need to bake some more cookies," Tamiko informed her, and I realized that we had not told Mom about our ice cream sandwich idea.

Mom looked puzzled. "Did you make a lot of cookie mix-ins? Those should have lasted all week."

"Well, we actually came up with a new menu item," I said, and I told her the story, from #savethecookies to Sierra's comment, to our sale to the high school business club.

"Whoa!" Mom said. "That's . . . that's great. I can't believe I didn't think of making ice cream sandwiches sooner. That means I'll have to bake more cookies tomorrow, but . . . it's okay. I'll find the time. It's worth it."

"We made great tips today," Sierra reported, and Tamiko and I walked over to her to get our shares.

"Yes!" I exclaimed. I had enough for the dress! (Adding in the money that my mom had said she'd give me.) I hugged Sierra and Tamiko. "You two are the best. We are an awesome team."

"Absolutely!" Tamiko agreed. "Come on. Sprinkle Sunday selfie!"

We huddled together as Tamiko took the picture. Then we broke apart, but I didn't want to let them go just yet.

"Hey, I'm sure Dad would take us all out for dinner if I asked," I said. "He's already picking up me and Tanner."

"Sorry, Allie, but we've got play rehearsal," Tamiko said.

"We?" I asked, looking at Tamiko.

Tamiko shrugged. "Sierra talked me into working on the sets. I get to use an industrial glue gun!"

"Wait!" cried Sierra. "We have rehearsal today? What time? I thought we didn't have one today!"

"No, we have rehearsal at six. I double-checked the schedule this morning," Tamiko said.

A car horn beeped outside.

"That's our ride," Tamiko said. "See you soon, Allie!"

"Adios, *chica*!" Sierra said, and my two best friends left together. As happy as I was about having made enough money for the dress, I was sad, knowing that they would be seeing each other the next morning, while I would be alone with the clones at Vista Green.

CHAPTER EIGHT
SULKY SUNDAY

After Tamiko and Sierra left, there was a short lull in the shop. While I was waiting for my dad to pick me up, I realized I had some time to talk to Mom.

"Mom, can we go shopping tomorrow?" I asked. "I need to buy a dress for the dance."

"Sure, we should have time to swing by after dinner," Mom said. "What shop are we going to? Daisy's?"

"No, Glimmer," I replied.

Mom frowned. "Glimmer? Isn't that the fancy shop that all the teenagers like? I don't think we can afford a dress there on our budget."

"We can if we add my tip money," I told her. Then I called up the dress on my phone. "This is the one I need to get."

Her eyebrows shot up. "That is *not* an age–appropriate dress, Allie!"

I had kind of known that I would get that response from her, and I kicked myself for showing her the picture.

"Well, that's what I thought too," I said, hoping that my logic would impress her. "But Amanda and Eloise told me that every girl at the Vista Green dance will be wearing a dress like this. So if I don't wear it, I'll stand out."

"You'll stand out if you *do* wear that dress—just not in the right way," Mom argued.

Anger suddenly bubbled up inside me. "You know, *you* are the one who was so excited about moving and about me going to Vista Green," I said. "If you think that school is so great, you should let me dress the way everybody else who goes there does!"

Mom sighed. "Let me think about it, Allie. I've got a lot on my mind right now. I'll give you an answer tomorrow. Send me the link to the dress, okay?"

"Why should I bother?" I mumbled, and Mom would have called me out, except that was when Dad and Tanner walked in.

"Hey, Meg. Hey, Allie," Dad said. "Tanner and I were thinking of Chinese food tonight."

"Whatever," I said, still sulking about my conversation with Mom.

Dad raised his eyebrows and nodded to my mom. "Can we bring you anything?" he asked.

"Come to think of it, I'd love some wonton soup," she replied. "Thanks!"

"You got it!" Dad said with a grin.

You would think that seeing my mom and dad get along so well would make me happy. But at that moment I found it totally annoying. If they could be so nice to each other, then why hadn't they just stayed married? My life would have been a thousand times easier if they had!

I was quiet all the way to the restaurant, and while we ate our egg rolls. Finally Dad decided to find out what was up.

"Is something wrong, Allie?" he asked.

"Something? How about everything? It's just . . . so frustrating!" I said. "Mom wanted me to go to Vista Green, right? It's not like I wanted to switch schools. And there's a dance coming up. And every girl going to the dance is getting this certain kind of dress, and Mom might not let me get it. It makes absolutely no sense!"

Then I had a thought. "Could you get it for me? We could go to the store tonight. They're open until nine."

Dad shook his head. "I understand your frustration, Allie. This is a lot to get used to, and you kids really have the most adjustments to make. But when your mom and I divorced, we agreed that we would stand together when it came to our kids. So if your mom says no to something, so will I. And vice versa. Two houses but one united parenting front."

I sighed. "Why are the two of you still so friendly? Why don't you hate each other after the divorce, like some other people's parents do? I mean, if you get along so well, why didn't you just stay married and make it easier for us?"

Dad blinked a few times. "Your mom and I are both better off and happier not being married. I know this is hard, but it's a lot better this way. It's a lot of change, but change in this case is for the better. If you don't see that now, I know you will someday."

Someday, I thought. That seemed like a long way off. But I was sandwiched in the *now*, and the now was turning out to be awful. It just wasn't fair!

"Noodles!" Tanner cried happily as the server put a bowl of steaming soup in front of him, and I was quiet again as I ate my chicken and broccoli. Dad was quiet too. He started to talk a few times but didn't seem to know what to say.

I ran inside to bring Mom her soup, while Dad and Tanner stayed in the car. "Thanks, honey!" she said. The store lights were on in the back, and in the bright light I saw how tired she looked. I knew she'd be up late again, working by herself, and I felt a pang of sadness for her. I gave her a hug. "Good night, Mama."

She held me for a second longer than usual.

"Don't forget to send me the link to the dress, okay?" she said. "I promise to think about it. I know how it can be with these things, honey. We'll figure something out together."

As I left the store, I realized that I really, really missed Mom.

It was starting to get dark by the time we got back to the apartment building. As we walked up to the main entrance, I saw Amanda out front with a little black-and-white dog on a leash.

"Hey, Allie," she said.

"Hey, Amanda," I said. "Dad, this is *Amanda*."

"Hi, Amanda," Dad replied. He crouched down and patted the dog. "And who's this?"

"That's Oliver," Amanda replied.

"He is a fine-looking Boston terrier," Dad said. "You know, I had one when I was a kid."

I was surprised. "You did?" I asked.

Dad stood up and nodded. "Yes. Buddy was a great little dog."

Tanner piped up. "So how come we never got a dog?"

"Because your mom is a cat person, not a dog person," Dad replied. "And a dog is a lot of work. So I kind of became a cat person."

"But you're not with Mom anymore, so you can be a dog person again!" Tanner said.

"Tanner!" I exclaimed. He was technically right, but he sounded a little too happy about the divorce, if you know what I mean.

"I wouldn't mind getting another Boston terrier," Dad said. "Buddy was a great pal. A new dog could be good company."

"Then your dog and Oliver could be friends," Amanda said.

Oliver, on the end of the leash, was sniffing the ground and snorting exactly like a pig. He had an ugly-cute white face and short, droopy black ears.

Amanda turned to me. "He is so cute when he plays with his squirrel toy. Do you want to come see?"

I looked at Dad. "Can I?"

"Just for a little while, Allie," Dad said. "You've got school tomorrow."

"Yes, I know," I said sharply, and then I felt bad, because Dad had been nice to me all night.

We all took the elevator together, and Amanda and I got off on the fourth floor, where she and her family lived. When she opened the door, a delicious smell of food hit my nose, and I saw her mom standing at the kitchen sink. I couldn't help feeling a little jealous. Amanda's place seemed so much homier.

"Mom, this is Allie from school," Amanda said. "I want to show her Oliver's squirrel."

"I remember Allie from the pool," Mrs. Bailey responded. "Come on in, Allie. We just finished supper, or I'd offer you something."

"That's okay. I just ate and can't stay long anyway," I said. "But thank you!"

Amanda took Oliver off the leash.

"Come on, Oliver. Let's go to our room," she said, and I followed her down the hallway.

"Hey, my bedroom is in the same spot in my dad's apartment," I said. I looked out the window. "We have the same view."

"Cool!" Amanda said.

Amanda's room had pale yellow walls, and her bedspread had little daisies on it that I thought were really pretty. I noticed she had a bookshelf in her bedroom too, and that made me like her even more.

She bent down by a yellow fuzzy doggie bed at the foot of her bed and picked up a stuffed squirrel.

"Oliver, get your squirrel!" she said, and she tossed it up onto her bed. The little dog jumped up with amazing ability and started wrestling with the squirrel on the bedspread.

I laughed. "Oh my gosh, that's so cute!" I said. "Maybe it would be nice for us to have a Boston terrier too."

"We could take them for walks together!" Amanda said. "And set up playdates."

"Doggie dates," I said, and we both giggled.

Then the phone in the pocket of her hoodie lit up, and she picked it up.

"Oh, hi, Eloise," she said. "Yeah, I'm going to watch it. . . . Yes, we'll watch it at the same time! It's too scary to watch alone."

Then Amanda kept talking to Eloise about some spooky show they watched online, and I started to think that Amanda had forgotten that I was in the room.

"Uh, I'd better get back to my dad," I said, and Amanda nodded.

"Hold on," she said to Eloise. "See you tomorrow, Allie. Let me know if your dad decides to get a dog!"

I nodded good-bye, said good night to Mrs. Bailey, and headed up to Dad's apartment. I started to feel sulky again. Amanda was really nice, but she was Eloise's best friend, and so I would always be a third wheel with them. It wasn't like that with me, Tamiko, and Sierra. We had always had a balanced friendship. But now, with me being separated from them during the week, I wondered if I was heading into third-wheel territory with them, too.

"Lock the door behind you, Allie," Dad said when I came in.

"Sure, Dad," I said, and I moped my way into my bedroom.

Then my phone lit up with a call from Sierra, and I eagerly answered it.

"Hey, Sierra!"

But Sierra didn't respond. I could hear her and Tamiko talking. Their voices sounded a little distant.

I'd been butt-dialed! That's when you have your phone in the pocket of your jeans and you sit or lean a certain way and your phone dials someone. It's usually the last person you called. I considered yelling "You're butt-dialing me!" to see if Sierra would hear me, but then I realized that the apartment neighbors would hear me too. I decided to listen in.

"I mean, I know you like Victoria, but what is up with that skirt she's wearing?" Tamiko was saying. "You just don't wear flats with an A-line skirt, that's all I'm saying."

Sierra groaned.

"What's wrong?" Tamiko asked.

"Why do you have to always be so critical?" Sierra asked. "Who cares what kind of shoes she's wearing with her skirt?"

"I'm not saying I *care*," Tamiko said. "I'm just making a comment about fashion. I always say stuff about what people wear. You know that. It never bothered you before."

"I know," Sierra replied. "I don't know what it is.

It just seems like you do it more lately, or something. Or it's meaner than usual."

"Well, you have some annoying habits too," Tamiko snapped.

"Really? Like what?" Sierra asked.

"Well, for one thing, you hum," Tamiko said.

"I *HUM*?" Sierra asked loudly.

"Yes, when you're really busy—like when things get crazy on Sundays at Molly's, you start humming, or when you're studying for a big test. You hum! And it's annoying," Tamiko said.

"Sorry. I didn't realize," Sierra said. "Maybe that's because other people like it, or no one else has been rude enough to mention it to me as a negative thing."

I had been listening to the conversation, stunned. I hated when my friends argued!

"Hello?" I called out. "It's me! Can you hear me? You butt-dialed me!"

But they just kept arguing. I couldn't bear to listen anymore, so I hung up. I almost felt like crying. I should have been there with Tamiko and Sierra, smoothing things out. I could have joined stage crew or something and worked on the play with them. But I didn't go to MLK anymore. I went to Vista Green, a school where I didn't fit in. Or the only way to fit in was by looking like everyone else.

Weirdly, a haiku sprang into my head. I took my journal out of my backpack and started to write.

Life in the middle.
Sandwiched between two places.
Where do I belong?

CHAPTER NINE
FROG AND FROG

"Did you decide about the dress yet?" I asked Mom as soon as I entered Molly's after school on Monday.

"Oh, Allie, I haven't had time to think," Mom replied. "I had to get up extra early to bake cookies and make ice cream and plan for the birthday party on Thursday."

"Can you think about it now?" I asked impatiently.

"If you push me into giving you an answer, it's going to be no," Mom said. "So if I were you, I'd give me another twenty-four hours to think it over."

"Fine," I said, and then I stomped over to my corner table and started doing my homework.

I tried again the next morning, as Mom, Tanner,

and I ate cereal around the kitchen table.

"Mom, did you decide about the dress yet?" I asked.

"I seem to remember asking you for twenty-four hours," Mom replied. "Can you just give me that, Allie, please?" She rubbed her head.

I put down my spoon. "You know, maybe I won't even go to the Vista Green dance," I said. "That would be the easiest thing, since I won't fit in. As a matter of fact, I probably won't fit in at the MLK dance either. So I guess I won't be going to either of them!"

"Oh, Allie," Mom said.

I got up, tossed my cereal bowl into the sink, and went to the bathroom to brush my teeth. Tears stung my eyes. She just didn't understand! Or she didn't care. I didn't know what to think anymore.

I ran past Mom in the kitchen, grabbed my backpack, and didn't say good-bye as I headed out to catch the bus. I glanced behind me and saw Mom standing on the front step calling out to me, but I was so angry, I didn't go back. I realized she was going to be really mad because she had a rule about not leaving the house without saying good-bye and "I love you." Well, she had that rule for me and

Tanner. I could remember plenty of mornings when Mom or Dad had stomped out, pretty darn angry with each other. When I got to school, it seemed like everybody was talking about the dance again. I needed a break.

Once again I decided to eat my lunch in the library so that I wouldn't have to talk to Amanda and Eloise about the dress or my mom or my decision not to go. I curled up in a beanbag with a book, and Mrs. K. didn't even ask me to help her. She just nodded at me as she walked past, and I think she must have guessed my mood.

On the way to math class, Colin walked up to me in the hallway.

"So, um, Allie, you're going to the fall dance, right?" he asked.

I stopped, suddenly feeling confused. "I'm not exactly sure. . . ."

"Okay," he said. "I, um, I hope you go. Sooo, what's the next book review you're going to do? The deadline is next Tuesday."

I was glad he had changed the subject, because talking about the dance with him had been slightly awkward—but also kind of nice.

Maybe I should go to the dance after all, I thought. But then for some reason I pictured myself in a *Little House on the Prairie*–type dress on the dance floor, while all the other girls were dressed like supermodels and were pointing at me, laughing.

After school I was glad that it was Tuesday, my day to volunteer at the library. That way I didn't have to go to Molly's and talk to Mom. And I was even more glad to see that Noor had returned.

"I had fun last week," she said. "And I thought maybe I could help with the younger children again."

"I'm glad you had fun," I said. I nodded to two little boys sitting at one of the library tables. "Ian and Alex are on a Frog and Toad kick."

"Frog and toad? They like slimy animals?" Noor asked.

"'Frog and Toad' is the name of a series of books for kids learning to read," I explained. "You can read the book out loud, and then I'll help Ian and you help Alex try to read it on their own."

"That sounds good," Noor agreed.

I spent the next hour happily reading *Frog and Toad Are Friends* with Ian and Alex. They were the rowdiest kids in the group, and sometimes it was hard not to get swept up by their energy. I had introduced the series to the two boys a few weeks before, and I was secretly thrilled that they both loved the stories. The Frog and Toad books had been some of my favorites when I was little. Frog was kind and patient, and Toad worried about everything and could be a little dramatic, but they were the best of friends, and they always helped each other out.

Alex started losing his concentration toward the end. He kept on chatting about the new pizza parlor he had visited with his parents. His comment stung a little when I realized that I couldn't go on pizza outings with *my* parents anymore.

"I do not like pizza," Noor told Alex. "It is very greasy."

"WHAT?" Alex screeched. He pretended to fall onto the floor. "You're totally missing out! You have to go to this pizza place and it'll blow your mind!"

Noor smiled. "Thank you, but I think I am okay with disliking pizzas. Now, can you read the next page to me?"

Alex turned back to the book. I was impressed with how Noor had calmed him down. She had totally shrugged off the fact that she didn't like a food that practically everyone I knew loved. I wished I had her confidence.

"This was a very good book," Noor said when we were finished. "It made me think of my new friend, Mari. She is very kind like Frog."

"You made a friend already? That's nice," I said, with a little twinge.

Noor nodded. "We are going to the sixth-grade dance together. My parents both said I could go. I do not know any American music, but I am excited to meet new people at the dance. And I am wearing a new dress."

She sat back down at the table and took a notebook and pencil from her backpack. Then she started to sketch a dress with a long skirt, a collared neck, and long, puffy sleeves.

"It will be blue, and my head scarf will match," she said. I could feel her excitement, and it almost made me want to go to the MLK dance after all.

"That's a beautiful dress," I said sincerely. "I hope you have a great time. And I hope I will see you again next Tuesday."

"I will be here," Noor replied.

Then I said something that I felt like I had to say. "I'd like to be your friend too, Noor." I know it sounded corny, but it felt like the right way to say it.

"Yes, we are friends," Noor said. "Are you a Frog or a Toad?"

I had to think about that. "Mmm, maybe a Frog." I paused. Lately I might have been acting more like cranky Toad, though.

Noor smiled. "Then we can be Frog and Frog," she said.

I smiled back.

Then Noor and I said good-bye, and I hopped onto my bike and headed home to the beach house. The whole way, I kept thinking about Noor. She was so comfortable being Noor, if you know what I mean. She was living in a world really different from where she'd come from, but she wasn't worried about changing to fit in. She was just being herself, and she was doing great. She'd made friends, and she wasn't worried at all about fitting in at the dance—she was happy to be wearing a dress that she liked.

Can I just be myself, wherever I am? I wondered. *But then again, where am I? I'm still in two places.*

I could feel my phone buzzing in my pocket as I

was riding, but I resisted the urge to stop and check it. When I got inside, I yelled, "I'm home!" and found Tanner watching TV in the living room and Mom flipping burgers on the stove. Mom being home, dinner together at home—it was kind of like things were normal again, or whatever normal was these days.

"Hey, Allie," Mom said. "Dinner in a few. I'm glad you're home." She came over and gave me a quick hug.

"Great!" I said, noticing that she'd put a little emphasis on the word "home." "I'm glad to be home too," I said, hugging her back. I felt bad about stomping out in the morning. "Let me drop off my bag and I'll come help."

I dumped my backpack in my bedroom and checked my phone. I had a bunch of texts.

One was a selfie that Tamiko had sent, of her posing in her cross-country uniform.

Third place today!!!!!

Awesome! I texted back.

Sierra had sent me a silly meme of a cat playing with a balloon. I texted her back a whole bunch of hearts.

Amanda had texted me five photos of cute Boston

terriers, and I had a text from Colin reminding me of the next newspaper deadline.

Okay, so I had friends, new and old. That was good. And just then I realized that I'd called out "I'm home." Because I was. This was my new home. Or one of them at least.

I took out my journal and wrote a new version of my last haiku.

Life in the middle
The ice cream in the sandwich
And it's not all bad.

I decided right then that I was definitely going to the MLK dance, and the Vista Green dance. Staying home would just mean I would be sitting home by myself, and that didn't seem like any fun. Maybe Noor was right, and change could be good. I still had one problem to solve: getting a dress. But I had an idea about that too.

During dinner I talked to Mom about it.

"Mom, I've been thinking about the dress," I said.

"I have too, Allie, and I have an answer for you—" Mom said.

"It's okay," I interrupted her. "I'm not going to get the dress from Glimmer. But I still need to go to the mall. Can we go tomorrow?"

Mom sighed. "I need to work late at the shop tomorrow. Your dad was going to take you guys for dinner."

"Then he can bring me to the mall," I said.

Mom studied me. "I wish I could go with you, but I have to get everything ready for the birthday party on Thursday," she said. "We can see if Dad can take you instead. But do you promise you won't get anything too mature?"

"Promise," I said. "Besides, if Dad is with me, he won't let me get anything too short!"

Mom laughed. "Yeah, he definitely won't. Okay, Allie. I trust you. I'll fill Dad in, but I think he can handle helping you."

"Mom," I said. "Dad is great at a lot of things, but maybe not dress shopping."

"You're right," she said. "Okay, how about you see if Sierra and Tamiko can go with you? Does that work?"

I leaned over and threw my arms around her neck. "Thanks, Mama!"

Then I started chattering about what Tamiko and Sierra were thinking about wearing, and how at Vista Green they had a DJ and everything. Mom smiled as I talked, and I could tell that she was really listening, not just half listening while she tried to answer work e-mails.

"Oh, my baby girl is all grown up and going to dances," Mom said. She looked at me with this sappy expression on her face. "But I'm so glad you're acting like yourself again."

Tanner looked up from his burger. "Who else is she supposed to act like? That makes no sense."

I laughed. "You know what, Tanner? You're right!"

CHAPTER TEN
TOTALLY ALLIE

Thanks to a few texts after dinner, I arranged for Dad to drop off me, Tamiko, and Sierra at the mall after school.

"Tanner and I will be back here at five thirty," Dad said from the front seat of the car when we got to the mall. "And then I thought we could stay here and go to the Bombay Café for dinner. I'm craving vindaloo. Tamiko and Sierra, can you join us? Otherwise I'll bring you home."

"Are you kidding? They have the best samosas," Tamiko said. "I'm texting my mom right now!"

"I think I can do it too," Sierra said as she texted on her phone.

"Great! Have fun dress shopping," Dad said, and

we got out of the car. "And remember what you talked to Mom about. We trust you'll get something appropriate."

"Mr. Shear, are you giving fashion advice?" Tamiko said. I realized I hadn't filled them in on the dress drama.

"Don't worry, Dad," I said as we walked away toward the store.

"It's nice to go out to a restaurant in the middle of the week," Sierra remarked. "That's really cool of your dad."

"He takes us out to eat a lot," I said as we walked through the Commons. "I don't think he likes cooking very much."

"That's funny. My dad loves to cook," Sierra said. "Even more than my mom, I think."

"Your mom is the best cook, though, Allie," Tamiko remarked. "I really miss her chicken. You need to invite me over for dinner sometime."

I nodded. "I will, when things calm down for Mom," I said. "She's been really crazy with the new business."

"Well, I think it's really brave that she took a risk and opened a new business," Tamiko said. "Kai says that fifty-nine percent of all new hospitality-based businesses fail in the first year."

I stopped short. "Really?" I asked. "That sounds like a lot."

"Your mom is not going to fail," Sierra said confidently. "Tamiko shouldn't have said that."

"What? It's a fact. It's math," Tamiko protested. "And anyway, I didn't say Mrs. S. was going to fail. She is obviously *not* going to fail. Remember, she has *us* working for her!"

"And her business is going to explode after the MLK dance on Friday," Sierra said. "Once everybody tastes her ice cream, they'll be hooked."

"Yeah, I hope so," I said nervously.

"So, why aren't we going to that boutique in Upper Springfield?" Tamiko asked. "Glitter Glammer Glommer?"

"It's *Glimmer*," I corrected her, and I shook my head. "I'm not getting that dress."

"Thank goodness!" Tamiko cried. "That dress was awful."

"Tamiko!" Sierra scolded her.

"What? I know you agree with me," Tamiko shot back.

Sierra frowned. "Well, I do. But there's a nicer way to say it."

I'd been a little nervous about inviting Sierra and Tamiko to the mall. They'd been bickering so much recently, and they had sounded so upset during the conversation I'd overheard. But Sierra and Tamiko had both agreed to come dress shopping with me, so I wasn't going to press them about their argument. I hadn't wanted to go alone, and Dad had seemed pretty relieved when I'd asked if Tamiko and Sierra could go instead of him.

"Come on with me to Daisy's," I said now. "There's a dress I want to show you."

The night before, I had checked online for the dress I'd found a couple of weeks before, the one that Amanda and Eloise had told me not to get. But thanks mostly to Noor, I no longer cared about wearing the "right" dress to the Vista Green dance. I only wanted to wear a dress that felt like me.

"Ooh, I love this place," Tamiko said when we walked inside. "I have been eyeing a scarf here for ages."

"And they have the flowy kind of long skirts I

love. I think they're called 'boho skirts,' and they're on sale!" Sierra said.

"Can I please show you the dress first?" I asked. "I want to make sure they still have my size."

"Of course," Tamiko said. "To the dress!"

I spotted the dress hanging on the wall, and Tamiko and Sierra followed me to it—the pink-and-purple dress with a scoop neck, and ruffles on the sleeves and the skirt.

"Hmm," Tamiko said. "It's very ruffly. But it's totally Allie!"

"Try it on!" Sierra urged.

Thankfully, the store had my size. I went into the dressing room and tried it on. When I looked at myself in the mirror, I wanted to squeal. The dress was perfect. It wasn't last-year Allie, or MLK Allie, or Vista Green Allie. It was just right for the new Allie, the girl who lived in two worlds and was trying to make the best of both of them.

I stepped out to show Tamiko and Sierra.

"Oh, I love it!" Tamiko explained. "Those colors are great with your complexion. It looks much better on."

"You look beautiful, *chica*," Sierra said. "You have to get it."

"I'm getting it!" I cried.

"So, is this dress for the MLK dance, or for the Vista Green dance?" Tamiko asked.

"Well, actually, I'm thinking I could wear it to both dances," I said. "I mean, I love it so much, and what's the point of just wearing it once?"

"I'm not sure how cool it is to wear the same dress to two dances, though," Tamiko said.

"Who cares?" Sierra asked. "Just don't post it on SuperSnap, and nobody will know."

I considered this. "I'm going to do it," I said. "I just need to send a picture of it to Mom and Dad. Then I need shoes."

"Okay, but first I need to go check out those scarves," Tamiko said. "Meet you at the register!"

Mom texted back right away, **Beautiful dress for a beautiful girl.** Then Dad and Tanner came in and waited with me while I paid for it. Then we went to the shoe shop, but Dad had to take Tanner somewhere else because he threw a fit. "Shoes!" he groaned. "So many shoes. Ugh!"

At the shoe store I found a pair of pink flats that matched the dress perfectly. And the best thing was that after paying for the shoes, I still had some of the tip money I'd saved up.

"Where should we go next?" Sierra asked. "We still have some time before we meet back up with your dad."

Counting my extra money had given me an idea. "Can we go to the bookstore, please?"

"That is such an Allie answer," Tamiko teased, but she didn't argue. I knew that she loved to haunt the DIY section, looking for inspiration for her projects.

The bookstore was a cute little independent shop called the Book Nook. They had a tiny café in the front where you could buy lattes and sit and read if you wanted. Normally I loved to browse the shelves, but that day I had a specific book in mind.

I found the shelf marked "Series" and picked up the newest book in the Secret Sisters series. I was going to lend it to my new friend Noor so that she could read it first.

We walked around the Commons, and then we saw Dad and Tanner coming toward us.

"Who wants some Indian food?" Dad asked.

"Me!" Tamiko replied loudly.

We all went to the Bombay Café and ate potato-stuffed dumplings called samosas, and rice and chicken in a sauce that wasn't too spicy (except for Dad's, which was really spicy). And we laughed and talked, and it reminded me of the days when we all lived closer together. But the funny thing was, I didn't miss Mom. I mean, of course I would have liked her to be there, but for once I didn't spend the whole dinner wishing she were there and wishing things could be the way they used to be. And that was nice. It was just kind of the way it was now.

After dinner we dropped Tamiko and Sierra off at their houses. Then I realized something. I had gone to the mall right after school, and I didn't have an overnight bag for Dad's apartment.

"Dad, can we stop at Mom's house?" I asked. "I need to get my overnight bag." Dad had decided at the last moment that I should stay over.

"Sure, Allie," he said. Then after a second he said, "I'm sorry if it's making your life difficult, having to go back and forth between places."

I thought about this. It was kind of difficult. But Dad was saying this after he'd left work early in order to take me and my friends to the mall, buy us dinner, and then drive everybody home. He really was trying to make things easy for us too.

"It's all right, Dad," I said. And then I qualified it by saying, "mostly," because I didn't want him thinking that everything was perfect.

"I think we need a better system," said Dad. He was really into charts and systems, so I braced myself. But he just said, "Let's get each of you two sets of almost everything you need. I know that sometimes you'll still need to pack up clothes to take back and forth, but we can probably do a better job of keeping things at both houses so that you feel more settled."

Tanner piped in, "Like two game systems?

"Nice try," said Dad. "I mean like socks and underwear, pajamas, maybe even an extra pair of jeans each and sneakers. You should always have at least one outfit at my house so that you don't need to go home to get something."

I thought about what he'd said. "Dad," I said softly. "You said 'go home.' Is Mom's house our home?"

Dad pulled the car over and turned around. "No. No, I don't mean that at all. You have two homes now, one at Mom's house and one at mine. But the thing is, they are both your houses too. You will be at home in whatever house you're in."

"That's confusing," said Tanner.

"It is," Dad agreed. "And it's hard. And I know you kids are trying really hard. Soon enough it will feel more natural. You'll see. These changes will get easier for all of us."

I blinked hard because I could feel the tears coming. There was that word again: "change." Would it ever be easier to say good night to Dad on the phone instead of in person? It was quiet in the car as we all thought.

"Are we sleeping here tonight?" asked Tanner, looking around. "Like a campout in the car?"

"No," said Dad, laughing. "You'll sleep at home. But first we can stop at your other house so that Allie can get an outfit for tomorrow."

He started up the engine, and we pulled back onto the street. I looked into the other houses as we drove by. I could see families at dinner and watching TV, things we had all done together in our old house. Mom's house was dark when we pulled up. Wow, she really was working late at the store.

Dad opened up his car door. "I'll go in with you

and help you get the lights," he said, and I was glad. I punched in the code for the door, and it flung open. Dad stepped in and flicked on the lights. I ran up and grabbed some stuff, then paused. In Mom's room I left a note on her pillow. "Love you, and we'll be home soon. XXOO Allie and Tanner." Then I left the front hall light on so it wouldn't be totally dark when she came home.

CHAPTER ELEVEN

JUST CALL ME THE REFEREE

Friday came, and I was so excited for the MLK dance that I could barely concentrate in school all day. I had been so focused on getting the right dress for the Vista Green dance that I honestly hadn't thought that much about the MLK dance. Now I couldn't wait to see my old friends—not just Tamiko and Sierra, but all of my classmates from sixth grade. I was a little worried that they wouldn't remember me or wouldn't care that I was there, but I was just happy to be able to go with Tamiko and Sierra, kind of like old times. During lunch Amanda and Eloise kept talking about the Vista Green dance, but I definitely wasn't feeling the same amount of excitement for that one.

"Did you get your dress at Glimmer?" Eloise asked me eagerly.

I shook my head. "No," I said. "It was too expensive, and I wasn't feeling it anyway."

I expected her and Amanda to give me a hard time, but they didn't.

"Oh," Eloise said, and then she and Amanda looked at each other, like they were communicating some best-friend thought.

They're probably thinking that I'm going to look ridiculous and that they won't want to hang out with me, I thought. *Oh well.*

Colin, at least, was acting normally. "So, I asked Lucy to cover the dance for the newspaper," he was saying. "And Nathan's going to take photos. I'm just trying to think of an interesting angle. Any ideas?"

"You mean, like, what people are wearing?" I asked.

"No, something more interesting than that," he said. "Like, maybe Lucy could ask people if they like to dance or not, something like that. I don't know."

"Do you like to dance?" I asked him.

Colin shrugged. "Sure, I guess," he said. "I mean, it's a dance, right? Shouldn't you at least try to dance? I don't get why lots of people just hang out by the wall."

"Maybe that is a good angle, then," I said.

Amanda and Eloise had been listening. "Don't worry. We'll dance with you, Colin," Amanda said. "Right, Allie?"

"Sure," I said, and I felt myself blushing again. Stupid cheeks!

I took the bus straight to the beach house after school, because Mom had asked Rashid and Daphne to watch the shop while she helped me get ready and then served ice cream at the MLK dance.

"The freezer in the van is all packed," she told me when I walked through the door. "I made Pumpkin Caramel Swirl, Chocolate Cinnamon, and Banana Cherry, to match the MLK school colors. That was Sierra's idea."

"Wow, they all sound delicious," I said. "How are you going to serve the ice cream?"

"I'm using the kiddie-size cups," Mom said. "I packed two hundred fifty of them."

"That's a lot of ice cream to scoop," I said. "I can help you, Mama."

"You are certainly not going to help me scoop

ice cream in your pretty new dress," she said. "I want you to have a fun night with all of your friends. No scooping allowed. Promise?"

"Promise," I said. I looked around. "Where's Tanner?"

"Your dad's picking him up from school," Mom said. "So tonight will be a girls' night with just you and me. I thought that might be fun. Hope that's okay."

I hugged her. "Actually, that sounds nice!"

After I took a shower, Mom sat me down in front of the bathroom mirror and blow-dried my hair. She rubbed in a special hair cream that smelled like lavender, and then brushed it out. She even added sparkly barrettes in my hair to keep it away from my face. I felt like a princess at the hair salon. And right before we left, she approached me with a tube of pale pink lip gloss.

"This shade goes perfectly with your dress," she said. "Do you want to try it?"

"I thought I couldn't wear makeup until I was older?" I asked.

"And that's still the rule, but it's a special occasion,"

Mom replied. "Old rules apply, but it's okay to make some changes now and then."

I nodded slowly. I understood she was talking about more than the makeup. "Okay. I'm in."

Mom applied the lip gloss, which felt kind of weird and sticky, but she was right—it did go perfectly with my dress.

"You look beautiful, Allie," she said. She stepped back and looked at me, and her eyes got all teary. "Oh, I wish Dad were here to see you." She wiped her eyes. "Hang on so I can send him a picture." She snapped a pic of me with her phone and zapped it to Dad. A second later she laughed.

"He wants to know what I did with his little girl, who just yesterday was riding a tricycle," she said, and giggled.

I rolled my eyes. Some things will never change. "Well, Mom, you look great in your Molly's T-shirt," I said.

Mom spun around and grinned. "Let's go turn some heads!"

We got to the school about twenty minutes before the dance started, so that Mom could set up. The

MLK janitors helped her carry her coolers into the auditorium. We followed them inside, and there were some teachers milling around, and a few students setting up for the dance—and then I spotted Sierra.

"Chica!" I called out, and I ran up to her. "You look amazing!"

Sierra had pulled her curly hair into a messy bun, and she reminded me of a ballerina, in a dark blue dress with sparkles on the top half and a wide, pleated skirt. Her blue flats had little silver sparkles on them too.

"Thanks, Allie," Sierra said. "Your dress looks even better on you now than it did in the shop. Hey, can you help me finish hanging up these stars?"

The MLK gym still looked like I remembered, with its gleaming wood floor and championship banners hanging high on the walls, near the ceiling. Sierra and the rest of the dance committee were decorating the walls with red and gold stars. The food tables set up had alternating red and gold tablecloths. Along with Molly's Ice Cream, Sam from Sam's Subs was setting up sandwiches on one of the tables, and another table held tubs of mini bottles of water. In the corner a DJ stood at a table behind two giant speakers.

As soon as we finished hanging up the stars, kids started to stream in. Tamiko made a beeline toward us. She looked totally adorable in a short-sleeved dress that was black on top, with a pink skirt that had a white cat appliquéd to the bottom.

"Thanks," she said when Sierra and I complimented her. "Mom showed me this online company that sells retro-style dresses. I added the cat."

"It is too cute," I told her. "You could have a side business, sewing cats onto everything for people."

"Cats by Tamiko," she said. "Hmm, it's got a ring to it."

I looked around at what the other girls were wearing. Some were wearing short, straight, sleeveless dresses like the ones from Glimmer. Others wore colorful dresses, or long dresses, and a few girls even had on dress pants, shirts, and ties. Definitely no clones there at MLK!

"Oh my gosh, Allie!"

I turned around to see a group of girls approaching us—Kyra, Victoria, and Claire, three more of my friends from sixth grade. They started hugging me and talking all at once.

"We miss you!"

"What's it like at Vista Green?"

"Does your mom really have an ice cream shop now? I need to go there!"

They made me feel like a celebrity, and I answered all their questions and then asked them some of my own, because I had missed them too. And then the music started, and things kind of got crazy.

Tamiko and Sierra pulled me onto the gym floor, and we started dancing.

Eloise loves this song! I thought, and the thought kind of surprised me a little. Why was I thinking about my Vista Green friend when I was at an MLK dance?

We kept dancing when the next song came on, and three boys ran up to us, holding cups of ice cream. I knew them all: Ewan, Connor, and Jake. A few weeks before, they'd had a stupid sprinkles fight in the ice cream shop and had made a huge mess. Only Ewan had stayed to clean it up, and to pay for the sprinkles.

Jake thrust out his ice cream toward Sierra. "Yo, this ice cream is the bomb!"

"Yes, it is," Sierra replied. "Please don't start throwing it around, okay? That sprinkles fight you had in Molly's was so immature."

"Yeah, that was dumb," Jake admitted, and Sierra looked surprised.

"Want me to get you some ice cream?" Jake asked Sierra.

"No, that's okay. I can get it myself," she replied.

Jake shrugged, and the three boys moved on. Sierra rolled her eyes. "Well, that was random," she said.

"I think that was Jake's way of apologizing to you," I said.

Sierra shook her head. "He could have just said he was sorry."

"Oh, lighten up, Sierra!" Tamiko said. "Let's go get some ice cream."

We walked over to Mom's table, and I glanced around at the kids in the room along the way. I recognized most of them, but not all of them. And except for Kyra, Victoria, and Claire, nobody else had said hello to me. Which wasn't a bad thing, but it made me start to think that MLK didn't feel like home anymore.

I also noticed that some kids were dancing, and other kids were huddled in the corners of the gym, or backed up against the wall. I briefly thought about

Colin's news angle, and then realized I was thinking of my Vista Green squad again.

"Girls, you look wonderful!" Mom cried when the three of us approached the table.

"Thanks, Mrs. S.," Tamiko said. "How's it going?"

"I can't scoop the ice cream fast enough," Mom replied. "It's a big hit. Especially the Banana Cherry. Making a flavor based on the school colors was a great idea, Sierra."

"School pride," Sierra remarked. "I think I need to try the Banana Cherry myself, please."

"Of course," Mom said.

"Me too, please," Tamiko added.

"How about you, Allie?" Mom asked.

"Pumpkin Caramel Swirl, please," I replied.

"No banana cherry?" Sierra asked. "Where's your school spirit?"

"I love pumpkin," I replied. "And, you know, it's not my school anymore. . . ."

"Nice going, Sierra," Tamiko said.

"Oh, Allie, I didn't mean it!" Sierra cried. "But you're here now, and it still feels like you're part of MLK, you know? I guess it was wishful thinking."

There were kids behind us trying to get to the ice

cream, so I motioned for us to move to the side.

"Come on. Let's people-watch and eat," I suggested. "I haven't seen most people here in a long time."

We found a place along the wall and ate our ice cream in silence for a minute.

Then Sierra glared at Tamiko. "You're looking at my hair! You hate it, right? Why don't you just say so?"

"I do not hate your hair!" Tamiko said. "I mean, a messy bun is not your best look, but I don't hate it."

"Aha! I knew it!" Sierra fumed.

This was starting to sound a lot like the conversation I had overheard when Sierra had butt-dialed me. At least this time I could help.

"Okay, guys, what gives?" I asked.

They both started talking at once.

"She says I'm overly critical!" Tamiko blurted out.

"She says I'm annoying when I hum!" Sierra said.

"You are!"

"No, I'm not!"

I couldn't help it—I laughed. "Come on, guys. You're both right!" I said. "Tamiko, you know you love to comment on what everybody's wearing. And that's okay, as long as the person involved never hears it."

"I could not agree more," Tamiko said.

"And, Sierra, I hate to break it to you, but you do hum a lot," I said. "I think it's kind of cute, but I can see where it might get on some people's nerves."

Sierra shook her head. "I honestly had no idea!"

"Now, whatever happens, we're all still going to be friends. Even when we drive one another crazy. So it's not worth staying mad for too long. So will you two please hug and make up already?" I asked them. "You know you're going to eventually!"

Sierra and Tamiko stared at each other for a minute. Then they both burst out laughing.

"Okay, hummingbird," Tamiko said.

"Fashion police!" Sierra shot back, and they hugged.

Then they turned to me.

"Thanks, Allie," Sierra said. "Tamiko and I always used to annoy each other once in a while, but it's happening a lot more lately. I think it's because you're not here to balance us out."

"Yeah," Tamiko agreed. "We need you, Allie. I wish you could come back to MLK."

A few days before the dance, I might have chimed

in with, "Me too!" But instead I said, "I am always with you guys in spirit. And you can always text me if you need me!"

"Right," Sierra said. "But hopefully we won't need you to referee for us again for a long time."

At that moment two girls walked past us.

"Is she really wearing pink shoes with a yellow dress?" Tamiko asked, making a face, and Sierra elbowed her.

"Really?" Sierra asked.

I took the empty ice cream cups from them and tossed them into the garbage.

"Come on. Let's dance," I said, and we went back onto the dance floor.

I had fun that night, and I danced so much that my feet hurt when I climbed into bed. Mom made some hot cocoa when we got home, and we stayed up late and talked about the dance, like what dresses we'd liked and what songs had been great for dancing. It felt nice and cozy in a way that I hadn't felt in a long time. In bed I cuddled up with Diana, my cat, but I didn't fall asleep right away. I stayed up for a while, thinking about things.

I don't belong at MLK anymore, I realized. It wasn't

that I'd felt weird or anything, but everybody at MLK had moved on without me. And I had moved on too, whether I liked it or not. Changes. Noor might have been onto something. Change was sometimes okay.

I realized something else. I was actually looking forward to the Vista Green dance. I just hoped I could make it through two dances in two days!

CHAPTER TWELVE
TAKE TWO

The next morning Mom hand-washed my dress, and it looked like new again. I put my flats back on, and Mom helped with my hair and supervised while I applied a little more pink lip gloss, and I was ready to go when Dad picked me up. He wanted to take me to the Vista Green dance since he hadn't been there for the MLK dance.

"Allie, you look so grown-up!" Dad said.

"Yeah, you look nice," Tanner piped up from the back seat.

I couldn't believe my ears. Had my bratty brother just complimented me?

"Thanks, guys," I said.

"I'm glad I don't have to go to a dumb dance,"

Tanner said. "Dad's taking me to the movies."

"I'm sure the dance will not be dumb, Tanner," Dad said as we pulled up to Vista Green. "I'll pick you up at nine, Allie, okay? Have fun!"

"Thanks, Dad," I said, and I got out and walked up to the school entrance. Suddenly I started to feel nervous. Every girl I could see was wearing a sleeveless, short Glimmer dress in silver, gold, white, or black. I really stood out in my pink-and-purple dress. Then I remembered how Eloise and Amanda had exchanged that weird look when I'd told them I wasn't going to wear a clone dress.

My palms started to sweat. I was sure I was going to be mocked, or even worse, completely ignored. Dad wouldn't be back for hours, and I'd be trapped at the dance, standing by myself, with nobody to talk to.

I walked into the gym and looked around. The dance committee at Vista Green had gone for a star theme too, but the decorations were a lot fancier. Constellations shone on the gym ceiling, and strands of silver stars had been hung from the rafters. It looked pretty, but I didn't see Amanda, Eloise, or Colin—just a sea of clones.

Then Blair, Palmer, and Maria walked past me—
then stopped.

"Nice ruffle dress, Allie," Blair said, her voice
dripping with sarcasm.

"Pretty in pink," Palmer hissed. "Not!"

They walked off before I could give them a witty
reply—which was a good thing, because I didn't have
one.

Panicked, I reached for my phone in the little
purse Mom had let me borrow. I was ready to call
Dad and tell him to come back and get me. But I
stopped when I heard Amanda call out to me.

"Allie! You're here!"

I spun around and saw Amanda and Eloise, and
I almost gasped. They weren't dressed like clones!
Eloise wore a red dress with a wide skirt that fell to
below her knees, and Amanda's sleeveless, pale blue
dress had a fluffy skirt on the bottom.

"Wow, I love your dresses!" I said. "But I thought
you were going to get yours at Glimmer?"

"Well, my mom said the clone dress was too
mature," Amanda confessed. "I was trying to talk her
into it, but then when you said you weren't getting a
clone dress, I figured I shouldn't bother."

"Really?" I asked, surprised.

"Yeah, and those Glimmer dresses were just too short," Eloise said. "I like a skirt that you can twirl around in."

She spun around, and her skirt twirled around her. Amanda and I copied her, laughing.

Then I heard a voice behind me.

"You look nice."

I stopped spinning and saw that it was Colin! He was wearing black pants with a short-sleeved white shirt and a red bow tie.

"Thanks," I said, smiling at him. "You do too."

At that moment the lights dimmed and music started playing. Colin and I looked at each other awkwardly for a moment. Were we supposed to dance together?

Rather than find out, I started chatting a mile a minute. "Wow, this is really different from the MLK dance I went to last night," I said. "I mean, they had star decorations too, but red and gold, the school colors, and not as fancy. But the music is kind of the same. Is that the same DJ? It might be. It kind of looks like him. Wow, I wonder if that's the same DJ? That would be weird, right? Well, maybe not, because how many DJs are there around here, after all? Probably not a lot."

Stop talking about the DJ! I scolded myself. But Colin just stood there, nodding and smiling, like I wasn't babbling on like a weirdo.

Suddenly I felt very shy. But why? Because of Colin? My palms started to sweat again.

"I was going to get a cookie. Do you want one?" Colin asked me.

"Sure," I said, even though my stomach felt fluttery.

Colin left to get the cookies, and then Amanda leaned in to me. "He liiikes you!" she teased in a sing-songy voice. I blushed.

"We're just friends," I said, shrugging. But I wasn't 100 percent sure I believed that. And that felt nice and weird at the same time.

Colin came back with the cookies, and we talked some more—not about the DJ, thank goodness. And then the four of us went out on the dance floor and started dancing. Twirling around on the dance floor, I definitely saw a few others who were not dressed like clones.

Potential friends? I wondered. Why not?

The beat picked up, and Eloise started jumping up and down.

"I love this song!"

"Me too!" Amanda and I said at the same time.

I took out my phone and motioned for Colin to get closer. "Come on, guys. We need a selfie!"

I snapped the photo and then, while I was dancing, sent it to Sierra and Tamiko.

Having fun! Wish u were here!

❤, Sierra replied.

Go, Allie! Tamiko texted back. **C u 2 morrow on Sprinkle Sunday!**

Thinking about Sprinkle Sunday reminded me of our ice cream sandwich special. Yes, being the ice cream in the middle was pretty sweet. I mean, that was the best part of the sandwich. And it held it all together. But the cookies on either side were delicious too. It wasn't bad being part of two different worlds. It could get a little messy sometimes, sure, but life could be a little messy.

"Allie, put down that phone and dance with us!" Eloise cried.

I slipped the phone back into my purse and joined my friends.

The next day was Sprinkle Sunday, but that night I still had some dancing to do! Just then a haiku came into my head that actually made me smile:

New things all around
The ice cream in the middle
Change is sometimes good.

Then I hit the dance floor.

DON'T MISS BOOK 5:

SPRINKLES BEFORE SWEETHEARTS

"Lunch is gross today," I said, lifting a piece of limp iceberg lettuce and letting it drop to my plate. I sighed and rubbed my eyes.

"Why so cranky?" asked my bestie Sierra as she chomped on some dry-looking carrot sticks.

I sighed. "I stayed up too late last night watching the World Series. My team wasn't in it, but I love post-season baseball, so my mom let me stay up. . . . Oh, oh, OH . . ." I yawned hugely, remembering to cover my mouth at the last second. "But then I couldn't wake up this morning."

"That's why you were late to class?" asked MacKenzie, my newer bestie. "Because of *baseball*?" Her bright red hair was pulled up in a high ponytail, and it swung from side to side as she shook her head and faked her disapproval of me.

"Oh, shush!" I laughed and swatted at MacKenzie, who shrieked and ducked away from me. "The worst part is that I was rushing, so I forgot all this stuff I needed: my cross-country shorts, my idea notebook, my copy of *To Kill a Mockingbird*. What a hassle!"

"You *must* have been in a rush if you forgot your idea notebook!" agreed Sierra. She tossed her curly brown hair over her shoulder and smiled at someone behind me. "Hey, girls!" she said.

I turned around to see Margie and Emilia, two girls from our grade, bearing down on our table. I liked them fine—we were in art and science together—but they weren't my BFFs or anything.

"Mind if we join you?" asked Margie.

"Go for it," I said, sweeping my arm at the empty seats at the table.

"Thanks," said Margie, setting down her tray with a smile of satisfaction.

"What's new?" asked Sierra.

"Oh, just brainstorming about the midterm project we need to make for science," said Margie, looking at Emilia. Emilia nodded, but it seemed like there was something they weren't saying.

Sierra put her head into her hands. "Projects are the worst! I'm all thumbs. I hate making them."

I cleared my throat. "I love making them!" I said. It was true. I was all about crafts and DIY and would waaaay rather create a project than write a paper about something.

"What is your class's assignment?" asked Sierra. We were in different science sections, with different teachers.

"We have to make something that shows a concept or principle in physics. Mr. Franklin said our projects can't just look good—they have to be meaningful and actually work. We have to submit our topics next week."

Margie looked at me. "What are you going to do for yours?"

I shrugged. My fingers itched to start sketching in my idea notebook, but I didn't have it today, of course. "I dunno. I'm not sure yet." I wouldn't have given out my ideas anyway, but I hadn't actually had any inspiration.

Margie nodded like she was perfectly satisfied with my nonanswer, and then she leaned in close. "Well, we actually sat with you today, Tamiko, because we wanted your advice about something. Right, Emilia?"

Emilia nodded, looking down at her plate of yucky food.

"If it's something about art class, I cannot help you there. Mr. Rivera—ugh! That man is a robot! I have no idea what he is looking for—" I began.

But Margie was shaking her head. "No. Actually, it's about Carlo. Right, Meels?"

Emilia blushed dark red.

"Do you want me to explain?" Margie asked her. Emilia nodded shyly.

At this point I was getting annoyed. These two had sat down and taken over my conversation with my two pals, and then one of them couldn't even speak for herself.

"What's going on?" I pushed.

"Well," said Margie, pausing dramatically and relishing the moment. "Emilia really likes Carlo. They danced together at the dance last weekend. And it wasn't just a fast dance. They slow danced, too! Then Carlo asked for her SuperSnap, but he hasn't sent her a single message since then. So we're not really sure if he likes her or not."

"Aww, that's sweet," Sierra said. "Why do you like Carlo?"

Emilia didn't respond, so Margie elbowed her teasingly. "It's his dark hair, beautiful eyes, and dazzling smile, right? Anyway, what do you think? What should we do, Tamiko?"

I looked up, surprised. "What? *Me?* I don't have a clue. I barely know the guy. Why would he tell me if he had a crush on someone?"

Margie shook her head vehemently. "No, but what do you *think*? Like, what should Emilia do?"

I shrugged. This was so weird. *What am I, Dear Abby?* "Um, ask him if he likes her?"

"Eeek!" Emilia squealed, blushing an even darker shade of red.

"No!" cried Margie. "You can't just ask someone straight up like that. That's way too direct. And what if he says yes just because he's embarrassed? He's kind of shy. Then that would set her off on the wrong course."

I sighed. "I think if you want an answer from someone, you need to ask them a direct question. Why all the playing around?"

Emilia looked down and shook her head.

No one would mistake this girl for someone pushy, so I wasn't sure what she was worried about.

Margie shook her head. "Never mind. We just thought you'd have some good advice, Tamiko, since you seem to be in the know."

"In the know about what?" *See, Margie? Ask a direct question if you want an answer from someone,* I thought.

"You know . . . boy stuff," Margie answered. "You're cool and you have guy friends and you're always wearing cute clothes, so I thought you'd know stuff about crushes."

In the know? About guys? I had some good guy friends from the cross-country team, but I didn't have a crush on any of them. And it was true that I loved dressing fashionably, but that's always been for *me*—I wasn't dressing to impress anyone.

I blew my bangs up from my forehead in exasperation. "Just because I have fashion sense and can talk to anyone doesn't mean I know anything about crushes."

"Oh well," Margie said. "I guess we'll just have to wait and see if Carlo sends her a SuperSnap. Or gives some other sign that he likes Emilia."

"Good luck," said MacKenzie.

Emilia nodded. "Thanks for listening," she added shyly.

We wrapped up lunch, and then Margie and Emilia left to go track down poor Carlo somewhere near the lockers.

MacKenzie, Sierra, and I stood and went to clear our trays.

"That was weird," I said, still puzzled.

"Beautiful eyes? Dazzling smile? *Carlo?*" Sierra said, and giggled.

"Wasn't it funny how it's Emilia who has the crush, but Margie did all the talking?" said MacKenzie.

Sierra nodded. "Emilia's obviously really shy, though. Poor girl. It takes a lot of courage to admit you like someone."

Even so, I couldn't imagine being in such a state that my friends would have to do all the talking for me. I was no love expert, but I knew that it was better to speak for yourself in any situation, thank you very much!

I was excited to get home after school and grab my idea notebook. I always had an idea notebook going—there was a whole shelf in my craft room filled to bursting with my used notebooks. I packed them with sketches of projects or crafts I was working on; pictures ripped from catalogs, magazines, or newspapers; ideas for ways to customize things I already had, like clothing or furniture; inspiration for my part-time job at my bestie Allie's mom's ice cream parlor, Molly's Ice Cream; basically anything creative in my life. It's where I really let myself go. Being without it today had been like missing a limb.

I pounced on it in my room and slipped the clipped pen off the cover to chew on. I had to pen-chew when I thought. It drove my mom crazy because she always thought I was going to chip my tooth. Hadn't happened yet!

The science project was what had my wheels turning. It had to illustrate some simple physics concepts, like force, motion, and velocity. My mom had recently brought home a bunch of spools of colorful wire from one of the labs at the college where she works, and I'd been dying to use them. Now I thought I could put them to use for this project. But how? With my idea due next week, I had time to come up with something really cool.

I put my pen to paper and let it roam freely while I thought about other stuff. I doodled hearts as I wondered why everyone was suddenly talking about crushes. I mean, come *on*, we were only in seventh grade!

Looking for another great book?
Find it
IN THE **MIDDLE**.

Fun, fantastic books for kids
in the in-be**TWEEN** age.

IntheMiddleBooks.com

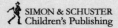